FALLING AGAIN FOR THE FOR THE SINGLE DAD

JULIETTE HYLAND

MILLS & BOON

First published in Great Britain 2020
by Mills & Boon, an imprint of HarperCollins*Publishers*
1 London Bridge Street, London, SE1 9GF

www.harpercollins.co.uk

HarperCollins*Publishers*
1st Floor, Watermarque Building, Ringsend Road
Dublin 4, Ireland

Large Print edition 2021

© 2020 Juliette Hyland

ISBN: 978-0-263-28762-2

Printed and bound in Great Britain
by CPI Group (UK) Ltd, Croydon, CR0 4YY

For Sarah,
who lovingly read my early works
and cheered me on.

PROLOGUE

ELI COLLINS PULLED at the collar of his tux and tried to relax as he walked toward his dad's study. The Collins Research Group Fundraiser was always a stressful event. At least this time, he'd finally brought Amara with him. For the first time in forever, he didn't feel like he was completely living in his dad's long shadow.

Despite the hectic schedules of his last year in medical school, and Amara finishing her nursing degree, they'd been almost inseparable. Amara made Eli believe he could be Dr. Eli Collins, not just the son of Dr. Marshall Collins. He could be as good as his dad. *Better!*

Eli had even spent last weekend looking at engagement rings. He'd agonized over the rings, waffling between two, unable to pick which one was best. After Eli spent an inordinate amount of time staring at each, the polite salesman had finally suggested he consider his options a bit longer. His younger brother, Sam, had goaded him all afternoon, enjoying Eli's indecision—something he couldn't quite seem to kick these days.

Though it wasn't Amara or marriage Eli was questioning. His professional goals had changed. *No*, altered. He was still going to be a doctor. Just not a surgeon—like his dad.

Eli pushed away the prick of anxiety at the base of his spine. He'd made his choice…he had. But Eli still hadn't found the right words to tell his dad.

His main objective hadn't changed: *be the best doctor.* But he doubted his dad would understand his choice of emergency room medicine when Eli had been groomed to join his dad in surgery. He wasn't questioning his decision—*he wasn't.*

And now his waffling was spilling over into other things. Eli wanted to marry Amara, wanted her to stand beside him and wanted to wake up with her in his arms each morning. Picking out an engagement ring and planning a proposal were supposed to be the easy part.

He'd never considered marriage before he'd met Amara Patel. His parents hadn't set the best example. Marshall was rarely present, and Eli's mother never seemed content. But that wouldn't happen to him and Amara. They loved each other too much. She knew his hopes and dreams, and Amara would cheer him on as he became the best emergency doctor in the city. And he'd never treat her as an afterthought.

The door to his dad's study flew open, and his mother wiped a tear from her cheek before offering her son a watery smile. "He's busy, Eli."

Dr. Marshall Collins was *always* busy. His dad was one of the top heart surgeons in the US *and* a genius inventor of medical devices.

The Collins Valve had drastically decreased the mortality rate of transplant patients waiting for a heart. Dr. Marshall Collins had one of the highest success rates of any transplant surgeon in the country. His dad's reputation was ridiculously impressive, and living up to it seemed almost impossible.

"What's wrong with Mom?" Eli asked as he entered the study. He made sure to get the question out before his dad could tell him what he wanted. Once Marshall started a conversation, he rarely let anyone get a word in.

Marshall's brows knit as he looked up. "Your mother?"

Eli sighed. "She was crying when she left." *How could he not notice that?*

If Amara had been crying, Eli would be chasing after her—not sitting behind his desk casually reading emails.

Rubbing his chin, his dad shrugged. "Your mother wanted to go on vacation at the end of the month. Greece, or maybe Jamaica?"

"Those are two very different locations." Marshall really didn't know where his mom wanted to go.

His dad's eyes narrowed slightly at the small criticism. "I wasn't involved in the planning, and the location is irrelevant anyway. I can't go. I have four patients that could get a heart at any time. I told her to take one of her girlfriends."

His dad always had patients that might get a lifesaving gift at any moment. It was his excuse for missed track meets, choir concerts and all of the other activities Eli and his brother Sam were involved in. Though he'd made sure to be at Eli's senior awards ceremony when he was honored as the class valedictorian. He'd even slapped Eli on the shoulder and told everyone that Eli might be better than him one day. That memory had carried Eli through the long stretches where his dad barely seemed to notice him.

But his mother mattered too. And she deserved

a vacation with her husband. "Couldn't your partner handle it?" If Eli could unask the question, he would.

The patient came first. That was a rule every Collins family member understood.

"Your mother knows I love her."

"You love her?" The question slipped into the room, and Eli was surprised by the tenderness that hovered in his dad's eyes. But it disappeared almost immediately.

"Of course." His dad's gaze slipped to the picture of his wife on the corner of his desk. "You can be a great doctor, Eli, or a wonderful spouse. Not both. Something always suffers." His father's eyes met Eli's. "And *you* will be extraordinary one day."

The rare compliment tripped along Eli's skin. He and Sam craved these moments. The smallest acknowledgments that their dad saw them— really saw them and their potential.

Eli stood just a hair taller as he asked, "What did you want?"

"Ms. Patel and I had a disagreement. She stormed off, very unbecoming." Marshall shook his head as he typed something on his computer screen. "You know how important what I do is. Make her understand."

Eli listened as his dad dictated the rest of his instructions. The Collins Research Group Fundraiser was a black-tie event designed to highlight the company's research and raise obscene amounts of money for a good cause. It was also his dad's evening to shine. The family always acquiesced to Marshall's demands for the night. *Always...*

He'd tried to prepare Amara for what to expect, as the Collins family could be overwhelming— even for those raised in it. But tonight's festivities needed to be perfect—then he'd be able to tell his dad about his change of medical specialty. Surely Amara would be able to put aside any arguments for one night—to make Eli's life easier.

As he opened the door to her suite, Eli saw Amara brush a tear away before she looked at him. Her small bag was sitting on the bed, and he tried to silence the alarm clanging in his brain. "Amara—"

"Did you tell your dad that you plan to go into emergency medicine?" she interrupted.

"What?" Eli blinked. He'd prepped his response for a complaint about his dad. His tongue was thick, and no other words materialized as she raised a delicate eyebrow.

"Did you tell Marshall your plans?" Amara repeated.

"Not yet. It will be easier after the fundraiser," Eli muttered. Tear-filled eyes met his, and Eli hated the reminder of his mother.

"Will it? Because he got you into the surgical residency program at Chicago Memorial Hospital." Amara raised her chin, but he saw her lip wobble.

"That's not possible. I didn't apply for any surgical residencies." Eli shook his head. Chicago Memorial was one of the top surgical residency programs in the country.

"I suspect most anything is possible for Dr. Marshall Collins," Amara countered.

"Maybe." Eli rubbed the back of his head.

"Are you going to take it?" Amara's question was barely audible.

His throat tightened. Chicago Memorial was the chance of a lifetime. "Maybe." The whispered word floated between them, and Eli's stomach dropped as Amara's lip trembled—again. "Chicago Memorial…"

Her dark eyes held his, and a touch of cold

swept across him at the despair he saw. Holding out his hands, Eli stepped toward her. She pulled back, and his feet faltered.

What was going on?

"Eli, you have to live *your* life, not his. You don't have to follow the script Marshall has planned for you." Amara hugged herself as her eyes pleaded with him. "Emergency medicine…"

"Is not surgery," Eli bit out, hating the defensive tone in his voice. "I'm the son of Dr. Marshall Collins. I have to live up to that."

"How?" Amara challenged.

Eli shrugged, trying to ignore the tightening in his stomach. Why was she asking this?

And why was her bag sitting on the bed?

"By making the *US News & Reports* annual Best Hospitals and Physicians list, like Dad." His dad had made the list for the last five years, and given Eli and Sam framed copies for inspiration.

"Your dad sleeps at the hospital a few times a week, even when he's not on shift," Amara argued. "He snapped at me for asking if he might be free to have lunch!"

"It's the week of the fundraiser," Eli told her. He knew Marshall slept only a few hours in the lead-up to the event and often ate in his office.

"And the last time I checked, he is still human, Eli. So, he must consume food," Amara bit out. "Are you going to work like that? Be that consumed by the hospital?"

"If that's what it takes."

And then his dad would accept him.

Eli's heart burned as that thought tore through him.

"At what cost?" Amara's teeth bit her bottom lip.

Eli felt like he was failing a test. "Meaning?"

"Are you willing to give up your dreams of working in the ER to be the best surgeon? Are you willing to give up my dreams?"

He watched another tear slip down Amara's cheek, but she didn't wipe this one away. That terrified him more than the lone bag on the bed, but Eli wasn't sure why. "You can come to Chicago with me. I want you to come."

Need you to...

"My father chases success too, and my mother stands by him through every crazy business venture, exciting opportunity and each new goal."

"Because she loves him." Eli stated.

Like you love me.

"That's what love is. Supporting each other."

Amara scoffed. "Really, Eli? I've listened to her cry herself to sleep. Where is her support? Or your mother's support? She's spent a year planning a vacation with your father. It's their thirty-fifth wedding anniversary, and she believes he won't come. Our mothers are part of the perfect picture of our fathers' accomplishments. They're both loving wives, but behind the perfection, they're sleeping in lonely beds."

"My dad saves so many lives." Eli hated his mother's distress, but his dad was right. Their calling had to come first. Amara would understand that. He'd held her after good and bad days during her clinicals. She knew what they did was important—*the most important thing.* "You're going to be a nurse—" His voice cut off as she reached for her bag.

Eli's mouth was dry as he asked, "What are you doing?"

"Going home." Her voice cracked as she laid a hand on his chest. "I'm not what you need."

"You are." He wanted to say more, but the words were trapped in his throat. His breath was ragged as he ran a finger along her cheek. "Stay, please."

"I love you, and I know you see medicine as

your calling. But I won't play the role our mothers play for our fathers, showing up to fundraisers or supporting the next big move, the next prestigious business or hospital. I won't pretend everything is fine while inside I'm dying of loneliness. Eli, you want to be the best doctor..." Amara paused, shrugged and added, "Or surgeon, I guess."

"And I will be, but that doesn't mean that we don't belong together," Eli pleaded. His soul was shaking as he tried to think of the right words to make her understand.

"I know what I want, Eli, and it has nothing to do with accolades and ratings. I want to be a nurse, but also a partner, a wife, a mother. And I want a man who will sleep beside me each night, raise our children, plan vacations *and take them—with me*. The patients are important, but so is family. Are you willing to put your family first, even if that means I may be the only one who calls you the best?"

He wanted to say yes. Eli's heart was begging him to scream it, get down on one knee, promise her all those things. But his brain refused to utter the word. Amara was right. He wasn't sure he could promise her that life, not if he wanted to be great—just like his dad. Her lips touched his, and the fire they always brought ripped through him. His soul cried out for her, but he let her walk past him.

Eli loved Amara, but his dad loved his mother too. Love wasn't enough to stop the hurt, and Eli refused to spend a lifetime hurting Amara. "I love you," Eli uttered the words, wishing they were enough.

He heard a soft sob as Amara pulled open the door, and he barely managed to keep his knees from hitting the floor.

"Goodbye, Eli."

Amara's last words tore through him, but Eli didn't let himself break. There was the fundraiser to get through, then he could spend the rest of the night mourning what he'd lost.

Spend the rest of his life trying to put the pieces back together.

CHAPTER ONE

DR. ELI COLLINS'S breath caught as he stared at the gaggle of new employees. The first night was always a bit disorienting for the new hires, and they tended to arrive in packs for the first week or so. A petite woman, with long dark hair, lagged behind the rest.

The graceful way she moved sent a pulse of need through him. *Amara?* He hadn't seen her in years.

And he wasn't seeing her now.

Still, Eli's heart pounded as he tried, and failed, to control his reaction to the miniscule possibility she was here. Hope, need, love, all wrapped around him before pain dismissed the fantasy.

Amara Patel was the best part of his past—and the worst. Any time he saw someone who bore a vague resemblance to her, Eli would stare for just a moment. It was never Amara, but after nearly a decade of trying, he still couldn't break the habit.

"The new crop of nurses and doctors start to-night." Dr. Griffin Stanfred slapped Eli's shoulder as he slid in front of him.

"I know." Eli shifted, trying to catch another glimpse of the woman. But she'd disappeared with the rest of the group. He wanted to run after them, force his mind and heart to realize that the mystery hire was just another look-alike. A beautiful, graceful, jet-haired woman, a talented nurse or doctor, sure, but it wasn't his Amara.

His—that was a ridiculous thought. Amara hadn't been his for nearly a decade. It was just a symptom of Eli's loneliness.

He had let his desire to be the perfect son of the great Dr. Marshall Collins cost him his happiness. At least he'd come to his senses before taking on a surgical residency he didn't want. That decision had been the right one, but Marshall had refused to speak to Eli during the entire duration of his residency and subspecialty training or the years that came after.

Only after Eli had given a keynote address at the second-largest emergency medicine conference in the country, eight months ago, had his father reached out to him. Their relationship was still more professional than personal, but Eli couldn't stop the hope that one day Marshall might finally soften toward him. If Eli just achieved enough…

He let his eyes linger on the staff lounge door for a moment longer. Eli took a deep breath. Amara wasn't at his hospital—*she couldn't be.*

She'd landed a job at a prestigious university research hospital a week before graduating with her nursing degree. And two weeks after they'd broken up. Eli had watched from the corner of the room as she celebrated with their friends.

He'd wanted to reach out to her, to tell her how proud he was, celebrate with her. But he'd worried that if he said anything, he would beg her to take him back. Instead, Eli had made his excuses and left the party. It was one of the many moments in his past he wished he could change.

But life didn't have a rewind button.

Eli hadn't gone into surgery, but every activity he did was weighed against what it could do for his career. How it would improve Boston General. Make the institution great. Get it noticed.

Get him noticed.

Because no matter Eli's achievements, he couldn't stop the questions about his father. Even when he was surrounded by emergency professionals, someone always asked if he was related to Dr. Marshall Collins. Their eyes inevitably widened when Eli admitted he was his son. And part of him evaporated as they peppered him with questions about his father's legacy.

You're enough...

Eli's soul lifted a bit. Even after all these years, Amara's voice still floated through his memories just when he needed it. That constant kept him sane and yet sometimes drove him mad.

Eli had considered calling Amara so many times. Just to check in, say hello. See if she'd like to catch up; if she'd gotten the life she wanted; if she'd moved on. But he couldn't, because if she had, then the tiny ball of hope Eli had never managed to extinguish would die. His heart didn't want to accept that final loss.

It was easier to imagine Amara in the ER than at home with a husband and family who loved her. *Safer...* They'd both believed emergency medicine was their calling. Even if he'd doubted it for a brief period.

"Gina quit. Took a job in Baltimore." Susan Gradeson, the ER's head nurse, sighed as she laid her laptop on the charging pad at the nurses' station. "Luckily, one of the new hires agreed to take her shift." Before Eli could ask any questions, Susan hustled away.

Boston General's emergency room had one of the highest trauma rates in the nation. It was used by physicians and nurses as a launching pad to one of the nationally ranked academic hospitals that dotted the city. If only they were recognized on that list, then maybe the other hospitals wouldn't have such an easy time siphoning away Boston Gen.'s talent.

Eli had been offered a position at several of those academic hospitals too. But he loved the chaotic nature of Boston Gen. He thrived on the constant challenges, and even took pleasure in turning down the jobs. He'd bring in the offer letter and let the staff help him draft a blistering no-thank-you note. Eli never sent those, but it was an excellent way to let his friends and colleagues blow off steam.

His cell dinged with an image of his niece, Lizzy. She was waving at the camera; her cheeks covered in chocolate pudding. Eli darted around the corner and video called his mother. She'd taken to the role of grandma the minute Lizzy was born. And she'd refused to allow him to hire a nanny when Lizzy came to live with Eli eight months ago. He didn't know how he would have survived without his mom's calming presence.

He'd never expected to be a father. Marshall hadn't set a great example, but Eli was doing his best. Which mostly meant Googling everything and hoping the mistakes he made were minor. His insides relaxed a bit as Lizzy waved again. Lizzy looked a lot like her father—a man she'd never remember.

Eli pushed his grief away. The months since his brother's passing had dulled the pain, but there were still moments where Eli had to remind himself that he couldn't call Sam after a hard day. Or text him a celebratory note after an unexpected success.

At least he had Lizzy.

"Hi, cutie!" Eli cooed as his niece played with the chocolate pudding on her high chair tray. Lizzy needed a happy parent, not a concerned, uncomfortable uncle who was still terrified that he was going to screw everything up.

He smiled and laughed at her silly antics as worries niggled at the back of his brain. Eli never wanted Lizzy to see how terrified he was to be a father. He may not have planned to be a dad, but he couldn't fail Lizzy now that he was.

"Did she eat any of that?" Eli shook his head as he stared at the messy, almost two-year-old.

"A bit." His mother laughed. "I was just getting ready to put her in the bathtub. Figured she might as well have some fun. Every kid loves to play with pudding at this age. I've got pictures of you and—" she paused for just a moment "—and Sam covered in the sweet stuff."

A nurse with dark hair passed by in Eli's peripheral vision. *Amara?* She'd already slipped into a patient's room by the time he turned to get a better look.

Why was his mind playing tricks on him tonight?

"Look!" Lizzy giggled as the pudding dripped off her fingers.

Focus, he reminded himself. Smiling at Lizzy, Eli shook his head. "You really are a mess—a cute mess."

"Daddy!" Lizzy stuck her tongue out at the camera.

Eli's stomach clenched. That title still felt off. Like he was robbing Sam somehow. "It's Uncle Eli, sweetheart."

"Daddy," Lizzy repeated.

"Well, I'm going to get her cleaned up." His

mom offered a soft smile, though he could see her blink away a few tears. "It's okay to be daddy, Eli. Maybe it's what she needs. Sam would understand—even give you a hard time about it."

"Probably." Eli agreed, then waved one last time before his mother shut off the video connection. Eli wasn't Lizzy's father. Sam was… always would be.

But he was gone.

He'd been killed in a plane crash along with his wife, Yolanda, heading to a surgical conference, just as Lizzy was starting to say her first words.

Like *Daddy.*

Daddy… It held so much meaning. Eli still felt lost, but Lizzy was his responsibility. *No*, she was his daughter. When she was older, he would make sure that Lizzy knew as much about her parents as possible.

Sam was the good son, after all. The one who'd followed in his father's footsteps, though he'd refused to take on any roles at his father's research facility after Yolanda announced she was pregnant. It was unfair that Eli was now the one putting Sam's daughter to bed, getting to watch silly pudding videos, planning her future.

And hearing the word Daddy.

When Sam and Yolanda had asked him to be Lizzy's guardian less than a week after her birth, Eli had agreed without thinking about it. But he'd never expected to take custody of Lizzy. He loved Sam, though watching him with his wife and daughter had always sent a wave of jealousy through him. But Eli's goals didn't include a family.

Hadn't included a family.

In the horrid days after the accident, Eli had held their sleeping child feeling devastated. But he'd sworn to raise her with all the love Sam had shown for her. Somehow, Eli was going to be both an amazing father and a top emergency room doctor. The patients *and* Lizzy came first. He could do this—*he had to.*

Turning, he stared at the room where the dark-haired nurse had disappeared a few minutes ago. Eli didn't think she'd exited yet. If a patient was being difficult, she might need help. That was why he was moving toward the room. Not because he needed to prove to himself that it wasn't Amara.

Just before he got to the door, Susan grabbed his arm. "I've got a kid in room 7 that needs stitches and an elderly man in 4 that probably needs to be admitted for pneumonia. Any chance you can clear either of them out of *my* ER?"

"*Your* ER?" Eli echoed. "Last time I checked, I was the senior doctor on staff this evening."

"That supposed to mean something?" Susan quipped as she marched toward another room.

That was Eli's running joke with Susan. The head nurse had worked at Boston General longer than anyone, and she ran a tight ship. Everyone fell in line when Susan Gradeson ordered it.

Eli looked over his shoulder one last time. But the nurse, or more likely, the figment of his imagination, still hadn't materialized.

He tried to convince himself that it wasn't Amara. *It wasn't.*

Eli had a few hours left on his shift. He'd see the dark-haired woman before he went home. Then his brain could stop hoping that a miracle had occurred. He had never stopped loving Amara, but that was a feeling he'd learned to live with.

Amara held her breath as Dr. Eli Collins finally walked away from the room where she was hiding. Her pulse rate was elevated, and she could feel the heat in her cheeks. Eli was here...*here*.

She'd already double-checked on the patient, a young woman waiting on her release papers following a minor fender bender. Amara had gone over the concussion protocol with her and made sure she knew the indicators for internal bleeding. Now Amara was hovering. Her stomach twisted as she tried to work out what to do.

She'd left Massachusetts Research after her relationship with Dr. Joe Miller had crashed and burned in full view of all her colleagues. No matter how high she'd held her head, there'd been whispers when Joe immediately started dating her ER colleague Kathleen Hale. Louder whispers when they'd eloped a few weeks later.

Amara had been considering a change for years. If Joe's affair was the catalyst for it, so what? But now she was facing working with another ex—and she'd never fully recovered from their breakup...

Amara was independent. That was the word she used to describe herself. *Independent*...that word sounded so much better than afraid of commitment. Terrified of losing your dreams to someone else's goals. Of disappearing in the one relationship where you were supposed to stand out.

That was the fear that had driven her to walk away from Eli. It had been the right choice. But it didn't stop the regret that sometimes seeped deep into her bones as she lay awake at night. They wouldn't have worked. It was the mantra she'd repeated for years. He wanted to chase glory, like her father. Eventually, that need destroyed everything it touched.

She'd watched her mother give all of herself to her father. All her dreams, her goals had been sacrificed to support him. And she'd gotten almost nothing in return.

Even after her mother was diagnosed with breast cancer, Amara's father hadn't put away his bid to secure funding for his newest startup. Her mother had fought for her life without her husband by her side. And it had been Amara holding her hand at the end, not the man she'd stood beside for nearly forty years.

The patient coughed, and Amara's cheeks heated again. The young woman hadn't commented on her extended presence—*yet*, but she was watching Amara count the supplies in the cabinet. Amara made a note to restock the extra-small gloves, and wanted to shake herself.

Coward! her brain screamed. She should march out of the room and pretend that Eli was just any other doctor on the ER floor.

Boston General was supposed to be her fresh start. Her new place.

And Eli was here.

Did he still have to look so handsome?

Amara hated the selfish thought. Eli had been gorgeous in college, and the last decade had been very kind to the man. No beer belly or receding hairline for him. No, he was still the tall, broad-shouldered, dark-haired medical student that had been every woman's dream date. Except now, he was an ER doctor. *Not a surgeon.*

Joy tapped across Amara's skin. Eli had evidently followed his own path. That didn't make it any easier to walk out the door and say hello, but she was surprised by how much it warmed her heart.

Amara once believed they'd grow old together. That they'd work in the same ER and go home to a small house with a couple of kids. It had been a good fantasy, and for a short period, she thought those dreams were enough for Eli too.

But what was a happy home life compared to medical glory?

Amara's heart clenched as she forced the past away.

What was Eli doing at Boston General?

She'd assumed he'd gone to Chicago. It was ridiculous, but every year she checked the online annual hospital report to see if he was listed with the other top surgeons. He'd wanted to be like his father so much, but working at Boston Gen. wasn't likely to land Eli on that list.

In a city full of prestigious academic hospitals, Boston Gen.'s administration wasn't interested in attracting investors that would make demands that took resources away from the hospital's patients. Which meant it was chronically underfunded in its quest to provide quality care. Eventually, many of its talented physicians and nurses sought out the hospitals with research dollars, beautiful new buildings and better hours.

The low retention rate for employees at Boston Gen. was well-known. It was one of the reasons why, when Amara figured she needed a change to jump-start her life, she'd applied here.

If she'd known Eli was working at this hospital… She forced that thought away. It didn't matter. Amara was not going to be another retention statistic on Boston Gen.'s ledger.

Squaring her shoulders, she marched from the room and ran directly into the head nurse, Susan.

"Sorry!" Amara grabbed her to keep them from tumbling to the floor. She instinctively looked over Susan's shoulder. Eli was gone—at least he hadn't witnessed her bout of clumsiness.

What would he say when they finally crossed paths?

Amara ignored that thought. She didn't want to think about Eli, now. Or ever, though there was little hope of that.

"No harm done…?" Wrinkles ran along Susan's forehead as she stared at her.

"Amara," she said helpfully. She'd stepped in at the end of their orientation yesterday when Susan had announced that the ER was short-staffed for this evening's shift. Amara doubted the head nurse had even bothered to write her name down before rushing back to her post.

She looked around Susan one more time and

then mentally chastised herself. Amara needed to get Eli out of her head.

"Looking for someone?" Susan raised an eyebrow.

"A doctor… I…no," she stuttered.

Amara suspected Susan knew she was lying, but at least she didn't press her. "While we have a lull, I wanted to see if you'd help with the health fair in a few weeks. All the hospital's departments have a few booths. Several of the ER doctors always run their own. There is a competition—the winner gets two extra vacation days."

Eli would love that. He'd thrived in competitive environments in college—always pushing himself to come out on top. But Amara hadn't been the right prize. She knew that wasn't fair, but a decade later, she still woke up from dreams where he was holding her. Her subconscious refused to give up the whisper of hope Amara was too scared to voice while awake.

Pain rippled up her spine, but she ignored it. Amara was starting a new chapter, and it did not include Dr. Eli Collins. Straightening her shoulders, she gave Susan her full attention. "Put me down for whichever booth needs help." Her voice didn't sound as strong as she wanted, but at least it was a start.

A man walked behind Susan, and Amara made sure to keep her gaze focused on the head nurse. She was not going to look for Eli again—*she wasn't.*

"You might want to get to know the doctors who are participating first. Like I said, this helps the community, but the competition..."

Amara waved away Susan's concerns. "It's fine. I don't need extra vacation time." Her father and his new wife lived in California now, and she had no desire to visit.

Not that she'd been invited.

Jovan Patel had barely waited until her mother was gone to set a wedding date. No long mourning period for him.

"We've got a four-car pileup coming in!" one of the nurses cried as she ran past Amara and Susan.

Susan turned and yelled, "Dr. Collins was talking to his daughter over by room 3, but he might be in room 7, putting in a few stitches now, and Dr. Stanford is in room 6."

Amara's insides chilled. Eli had a daughter. Perhaps even a wife. Her heart raced as she headed for the ambulance bay doors. It was her body prepping for the incoming wounded, not because of Eli.

How simple would life be if she could believe that?

Amara joined Eli as he raced along by the gurney carrying a child. There wasn't time for her to unpack any feelings. She had spent a year in her mother's sick room. She'd been her mother's rock, providing comfort and never letting her emotions show. Never breaking. She drew on all those reserves now.

If Eli was surprised to see her, he didn't show it. "Do you know how old he is, Javier?" Amara asked.

The paramedic shook his head. "Sorry, Amara, no."

"Tell me what we know so far," Eli stated as he guided them into an exam room.

Javier was already passing the child's paperwork to the admissions assistant. "He was in the backseat. Car crushed the driver's side door. He was behind his mother."

"The mother?" Amara asked quietly as she grabbed a pair of gloves. Her insides curled as the paramedic looked over her shoulder at the small boy.

Javier lowered his voice. "Meredith and Landon were bringing her in. She'll go straight to the operating room."

The paramedic's eyes hovered over the child again, and Amara saw him shudder.

"I don't know if he can give you any information, but you might…" Javier's eyes were downcast as he headed for the door. "I've got to get going, two more people were trapped in another car."

The boy's mother might not make it. That was the truth Javier couldn't bring himself to voice. The child couldn't be more than five. Amara's heart tore. She'd been an adult when her mother passed, and her life had altered completely.

What would happen if…?

"Amara?" Eli asked, his dark eyes moved between their patient and her.

"Nice to see you again, Dr. Collins." She could see the piles of questions buried in his stare. Or maybe she just hoped there were questions to match the dozens clamoring in her brain. This wasn't the time or the place for a reunion, though.

She offered him and their patient a smile as

she sat on the bed and started wiping dried blood from a cut above the child's eye. There was no reason to think of her mom now. It was ridiculous. If it wasn't for Eli's shocking presence, she was sure her nerves wouldn't feel so raw.

"I'm just going to look at your eyes." Eli raised his penlight.

"Momma!" The little boy screamed as he pulled at the collar stabilizing his neck.

The yell echoed in the small room, and Amara saw Eli's head pop back. He seemed as surprised by the previously silent child's outburst as she was. Amara slowly ran her gloved fingers along the boy's chin. The motion seemed to calm small kids. She wasn't sure why, but when you found something that worked in the ER, you used it.

"Dr. Collins and I are going to help you while some of the other doctors look after your mom." Amara nodded to the child. "Can you tell me your name?" She patted his hand as she carefully turned it over. There were a few scrapes on his palm, but they were no longer bleeding.

"Momma!" he cried again as his eyes moved between Amara and Eli.

Eli bent over. "Hi, buddy." He waved and stuck his tongue out too.

The action was ridiculous, and Amara had to force her mouth closed.

What was Eli doing?

The little one blinked and then stuck out his own tongue. The child let out a laugh as Eli made another ridiculous face.

Amara barely caught the surprised giggle from escaping her lips. Eli was apparently a pro at calming kids.

He's a father, her brain reminded her.

"Your tongue looks very healthy," Eli cooed. "Now, can you tell me your name?"

The little boy sniffed before pursing his lips and trying to shake his head no. When the child couldn't move his head much, he let out another wail.

"His eyes look normal, and besides the cuts on his forehead and chin, there doesn't appear to be any head injuries," Eli stated quietly. "Can you tell me your name?" he repeated. "We really need to know it, little man."

The child's bottom lip stuck out, but he didn't utter a single word. His small free hand pulled at the neck brace again. Then his eyes darted to the door.

Amara knew he was terrified, and she offered

him a bright smile as she got his attention. "You can't move your head until E…" Amara caught herself, but she could feel the heat in her cheeks. They were at work; she couldn't call him Eli.

"Dr. Collins and I need to make sure you are okay. Then we can take this big brace off."

When the boy still didn't say anything, Amara shifted tactics. "Let's play a little game. I want you to squeeze my hand once if the answer is yes, two times if it's no. Understand?"

One light squeeze pressed against Amara's palm. Eli—*Dr. Collins* nodded to Amara as she briefly glanced at him before refocusing on the little boy.

"I bet your mom tells you not to talk to strangers, right?" Another soft squeeze pushed against Amara's palm. "That's really smart of your mom," she stated.

Amara wiped more blood away from the cut above the child's eye. It was going to need several stitches. "Did she ever tell you that it was okay to talk to police officers or firefighters if you got lost?"

Another light squeeze and the little boy's eyes started to water. Amara wished there was a way she could put him at ease. If he would just give them his name…

Pushing a bit of his hair off his forehead, Amara patted his cheek to get him to look at her. "Well, we are helpers just like firefighters and police officers. I'm Amara, and I'm a nurse. This is Dr. Collins."

"Eli," he interjected.

His soothing tone washed over the room. Amara's heart beat a little faster. She'd always reacted to Eli. That hadn't changed, but she didn't appreciate it right now. "Can you tell me your name now that you know both of ours?"

"Ricky." The whispered response was barely audible, but it was enough.

"How old are you, Ricky?" Amara leaned closer.

"Five and a half." His lip trembled.

Eli grinned at Amara. The dimple in his left cheek sent a small wave of happiness through her. They'd been a great team years ago. At least that hadn't changed. "Ricky, I need you to tell us if anything hurts."

His blue eyes floated with tears. "My belly."

Standing, Amara squeezed Ricky's hand. "I'm

going to lift your shirt, so Dr. Eli can see your stomach."

Deep bruises were already appearing along his chest, where the five-pointed safety belt had held him in place. It looked painful but had likely saved the boy's life. As Eli slowly felt along Ricky's stomach, the child laughed, and Amara let out a breath she didn't realize she'd been holding.

"Ricky, I think your belly is okay, but I am going to order some pictures to look and make sure. Now I need to check the rest of you." Eli's gaze shot to Amara.

Was he happy she was here? Annoyed? Confused? There were dozens of reasons for her not to care. Dozens…

If only her brain could manage to produce a few on command.

Amara distracted Ricky while Eli finished his examination. She talked about her cat knocking her cup of milk off the counter and was rewarded with a tiny smile. These were the moments she lived for as a nurse. Making a patient's horrid day just a little bit better.

As Eli ran a pen up Ricky's foot, Ricky's toes curled, and the boy giggled. The little guy was probably going to be all right. *At least physically.* If his mom… Amara forced those thoughts away. Boston General was a good trauma center. Ricky's mom was in excellent hands.

"I have a dog named Ketchup." Ricky leaned toward Amara. "What's your cat's name?"

"Pepper," Amara answered without hesitation. Her cat had passed away a few months ago, but Amara still regaled people with his stories. After all, Pepper had been distracting patients for years. His antics had always made Amara laugh, and his snuggles had gotten her through some of her darkest days. Amara still sometimes looked for him when she entered her apartment.

"I think we can take the neck brace off," Eli said.

Amara kept rattling on about Pepper as she removed the brace, enjoying each of Ricky's giggles.

Susan rushed into the room. "The ambulance just radioed in. They managed to free the people in the car behind this little guy and his mom. What's the situation here?"

"Stitches needed, and I want an X-ray and an ultrasound of his belly, but Nurse Patel and I can see to that after."

Nurse Patel...

Eli hadn't almost called her Amara. Clearly, he didn't have any problem thinking of her as a colleague. But then, why would he? She'd ended it, but not because she didn't love him.

But he'd let her walk away.

"Ricky is only five." Amara voiced her concern. "I should stay with him."

"No!"

Eli's forceful command stunned her. Squaring her shoulders, Amara held his gaze. "Eli, we can't leave him alone. His mother..." She puckered her lips. Amara was not going to discuss the fact that Ricky's mother might not make it in front of him.

"This is Boston Gen." Eli crossed his arms. "We don't have medical personnel to spare. *If* you're going to work here, you need to get used to that."

If? How dare he? She wasn't trying to shirk any duties. They couldn't leave an injured child in the ER alone. What would happen if he left his room, or got bored and started exploring the room he was in?

Ricky could get hurt. Eli was a father. Surely, he understood her concern.

The head nurse stared at Eli for a moment before turning her focus back to Amara. "We need all of the medical staff focused on the incoming injured, Amara. I've called one of our volunteers, Stephen. He has four children and six grandchildren. He often sits with our little ones until social services or their parents get here."

An older gentleman bearing a remarkable similarity to Santa Claus stepped into the room with a backpack full of toys and a stuffed elephant. "Hi, little man."

"Ricky," Amara stated.

"Well, I'm going to hang out with you for a little while, Ricky." Stephen dumped a few toys on the bed, and Ricky's eyes widened.

Eli didn't wait for Amara to follow him. That shouldn't hurt. This was just a job, and, if they were on opposite shifts, they could probably go weeks without seeing each other. Except this was Boston Gen., she reminded herself. If she stayed, Amara was going to be seeing a lot of Eli.

She could do this—*she had to.*

Amara took a deep breath and then marched from the room. If he didn't like her presence here, then Eli could seek new employment. Amara was not going to run.

CHAPTER TWO

SHE WAS HERE. Eli's brain tried to focus as his soul screamed with joy. He wanted to believe his heart was racing from the adrenaline of the emergency, but he knew that wasn't the reason.

Amara was here.

He needed to find a way to keep his emotions in check.

Why had he shouted at her?

Eli wanted to kick himself, but there wasn't time. He hadn't been lying; they didn't have the medical staff to spare with two more critical patients arriving. But he'd demanded Amara come with him because Eli was terrified that if he blinked, she might disappear.

He had no idea why Amara had chosen Boston Gen., but for however long she stayed, she'd be an asset. And he'd see her almost every day. Eli clamped down on the excitement that brought. Amara was kind, intelligent and gorgeous. She was probably happily married with a couple of kids. Which meant working with her was going to be a dream.

And a nightmare.

He'd been impressed with how she'd calmed Ricky, quiet, authoritative and comforting. Eli's interactions with children still felt a bit stilted to him. Like he was an actor pretending. Even with Lizzy, Eli worried that he wasn't showing her enough affection. He never wanted Lizzy to think that she had to earn his love.

Like he'd had to with his own father.

Dr. Griffin Stanfred was already paired with Renee, another nurse, as the first patient rolled through the door. The elderly woman was covered in blood but conscious as Griffin took her into a trauma room.

Javier, the paramedic who delivered Ricky earlier, raced through the glass doors with the other patient. "Crushed legs, head trauma. He's coded once already."

Amara grabbed the other side of the gurney as they headed for trauma room 2. Her face tightened as she listened to Javier describe the injuries. Her dark eyes met his, and Eli knew what she was thinking. Their odds of saving this patient were slim.

Some nights he hated his job.

Susan and two other nurses were waiting for them in trauma room 2. Before they could get him transferred to the hospital gurney, the patient started coding again. Eli initiated CPR.

Amara fit seamlessly into the hectic room. It took over an hour, but they managed to stabilize the patient enough to get him up to surgery. Eli leaned against the door of the trauma room as he watched the surgery nurses rush him off. The man had a collapsed lung and internal bleeding, wounds that on a healthy man might be fatal, but given his age…

Eli sighed. Some nights the ER was filled with infected scratches, burns and coughs. Things that, if people had the resources, they could get treated at their family physician before it needed emergency care. Those nights were horribly dull. He'd take a million of them over the chaos of treating patients he knew were unlikely to survive.

"You okay?" Amara's soft question hung in the quiet trauma room as she put away the last of the supplies.

For just a moment, Eli wanted to tell her the truth. Wanted to shout, *No!*

His life had been crazy—was still crazy. In the last year, he'd gone from being a single professional who spent so much time at the hospital that he'd killed half a dozen easy-to-raise house plants, to a single father.

The transition was terrifying, and as Eli stared into Amara's large brown eyes, his soul begged him to unload a bit of its burden. Explain all the new fears that had materialized when fatherhood was thrust upon him.

Amara had been his safe space once. The keeper of his secrets. The person who listened to all his dreams and never questioned why he wanted a different path from that of his father. Who saw him as Eli, not the son of Dr. Marshall Collins. It would be so easy to pretend that she was asking more than a simple question after a difficult patient. But she was his colleague now, nothing more.

His heart shuddered, but Eli forced himself to nod. "I'm fine." He wanted to say how much he'd missed her; how he wished he'd kept her close all those years ago. His chest seized as he stared at her. She was really here, less than three feet from him.

Amara raised an eyebrow and shook her head.

"Not sure I believe you." Her eyes searched his face, but she didn't push him further.

Before she could walk away, Eli added, "Thanks for checking. But I *am* fine. Just stunned to find myself coming down from an adrenaline rush next to you. Sorry I yelled earlier. That was unprofessional and uncalled for."

Amara nodded. "Thank you."

Eli crossed his arms and tried to think of something other than kissing her. "I still can't believe you're actually at Boston Gen." Amara's dark eyes met his, and for just a moment, Eli felt like he was home again. But Amara wasn't home anymore. He'd given that up when he let her go.

"I'm the one that should be surprised!" Amara let out a soft chuckle. "What is Dr. Eli Collins doing at Boston Gen.? And in the ER!" She winked as she leaned against the other side of the door.

Was she intentionally putting distance between them?

"I told my father I wasn't going to be a surgeon the day after you left…" Eli felt his cheeks heat as Amara's lips slipped open.

Did she wish Eli had called her after that?

He'd thought about it, so many times… "He…

uh…didn't take it well." An uncomfortable laugh escaped Eli's lips. Marshall's response still made him wince after all these years.

Amara's hand reached for him, but she pulled it back. "I'm sorry, Eli."

"Don't be. This is where I belong," he said. It had hurt, still hurt, to realize that his father might never see his successes as worthy. But the ER was Eli's second home.

"Yes, it is." Her smile was radiant in the small space between them.

For the millionth time, he wished he could have figured where he belonged before Amara had walked away. But that hadn't been the only issue to come between them. All the women he'd dated since Amara had complained that he was married to his job. And he was—or had been before Lizzy came to live with him.

Now he was trying to figure out his plans to advance the reputation of Boston General's ER and be a present dad for Lizzy. *Balance* was his new mantra; he could manage that even if Marshall had failed. What would Amara think if she knew he was committed to being home as much as possible?

He pushed away the hope pressing against his

heart. "Why are you here, Amara? Why Boston Gen.?"

"I needed a change." Her eyes rotated from his to the floor, and she wrapped her arms tightly across her chest.

What had happened?

He managed to keep the question buried. She didn't look like she'd appreciate it. "Well, Boston Gen. will definitely be that. The pace here is often chaotic. We're understaffed and serve a higher proportion of the uninsured than any of the other hospitals. Some nights it's downright crazy. But with a few changes, we could be the top place in the city, Amara."

As her name slipped from his lips, his heart begged him to tell her how much he'd enjoyed this little interlude, ask her if she'd like to grab a cup of coffee. Or if she still preferred tea. But Eli locked those words away.

"Thanks for the warning." Sliding away from the wall, she said, "I can handle it, Eli."

"I have no doubt about that."

Amara nodded before she walked away.

Her shoulder almost brushed his as she headed to the nurses' station. Eli wished she'd touched him, even a brief accidental touch.

God, he'd missed her.

It had taken him nearly a year to feel like himself again after she'd ended things. No, Eli amended; he'd never felt quite whole again. Instead, he'd learned to deal with a missing part of his heart. But Eli still felt the hospital and the patients were his ultimate priority.

He was learning to balance things with Lizzy, but he was a doctor first—*always*. And one day, he was going to be in that annual report of the best physicians. But reminding himself of that did nothing to stop the yearning for Amara.

Eli just needed to get through this shift.

But she'd be here tomorrow too and the day after that.

Amara's soft scent spun through him, and Eli told himself to stop being ridiculous. It was the memory of how she'd smelled, how she felt, how she made him feel, that was chasing him now.

Nothing more.

Could he work with her? Eli shook the question away. Of course, he could. Amara was an excellent nurse, and she'd be an asset to the hospital, that was all that mattered.

His gaze wandered to the nurses' station. She

was here. As a colleague, his brain ruthlessly reminded his heart. But it didn't care.

Amara yawned as she signed off on a few case reports. The rest of her shift had been blessedly quiet, and she and Eli had managed to avoid each other for most of the night. That should make her happy, or at least it should be a neutral feeling. But Amara had found herself looking for him countless times.

Even with Eli's unexpected presence, Amara had had a good night. Here at Boston Gen. she'd just been Amara. No one had asked how she was doing. No one questioned if she was feeling lonely or offered to set her up with someone. No one commented on how Joe wasn't good enough for her, while also asking if she'd heard about his impending parenthood.

She'd tried to be grateful to everyone in her last hospital for their concern, but she'd felt like a fool there. Here the only hiccup was Eli.

Amara's chest hurt as she remembered their brief conversation. She'd almost confided how much she'd missed him. How glad she was that he hadn't taken the surgical residency his father had sought for him. She hadn't lied; Eli did belong in the ER. But his comment that Boston Gen. could be the best in the city with only a few changes had sent a chill down her spine.

Eli was clearly still worried about that annual report—the recognition he thought he needed. Still measuring success by a metric his father had laid out.

Boston General didn't need fixing. Part of what made this hospital so special was that it focused only on its patients, not fundraising, recognition, or awards. It just served the community—and it was a shame that it didn't earn the respect it should. At least that was Amara's opinion.

She looked around one more time but then shook herself. She shouldn't be searching for him, hoping they would work on the same shift, shouldn't be focused on him at all. Still, after they'd worked on their last patient, Eli had seemed a little lost. Her palms had itched to reach for him. At least she'd managed to avoid that urge. It wasn't professional. But for all the confidence he exuded, Amara still saw the insecurity in him. And maybe loneliness too.

Or maybe she was just exhausted. Eli had a daughter, a family. There was no reason for him to be lonely. Amara was starting over, and that meant looking forward—not back.

It had hurt to walk away when she'd loved him so much. But she'd wanted a partner, a true partner. Someone who didn't chase business deals or national rankings while skipping dinner, vacations and recitals with their family.

She couldn't live in her partner's shadow. Joe had claimed she hadn't really needed him. That she'd made decisions without considering him. That he'd had to cheat on her. *Had to.* But if you needed someone, they could destroy you.

Amara flinched at the intrusive thought. She hated that she'd believed that was one way to protect herself from feeling like her mother had.

Like Amara had when she'd ended things with Eli.

She'd needed Eli, though she hadn't realized how much before she walked away. For months, years, her heart had felt like it had evaporated. Leaving him was the right choice back then; she'd loved Eli so much that she'd have lost herself eventually. At least that was the story she always told herself when the memory of what they'd shared chased her.

And she hadn't let herself fall that hard for anyone since.

"Amara?" Eli's hand pushed lightly against her shoulder.

"Eli?"

Her heart sang, then cried as he broke the connection. How was she supposed to work with him if she still responded to the simplest touch? Blinking, she covered a yawn.

"Sorry, did you need something?"

"You looked lost in thought." His eyes dipped to her lips. Eli opened his mouth to say something else, then closed it and shook his head.

Amara nodded and shrugged "Nightshift does cause the mind to wander if you aren't too busy with patients."

"Did it wander anywhere good?" he teased.

"Nope." Amara's cheeks felt hot, and she kept her gaze focused elsewhere, away from his dark chocolate eyes. Years ago, he'd have challenged the lie, but now Eli just raised an eyebrow. "Did you need something, Dr. Collins?" she asked again.

His lips turned down, but his voice was steady as he nodded toward the door. "Our shift is over. I wanted to make sure you didn't stay past quitting time." Eli waved to an incoming doctor as he started for the elevators.

After grabbing her purse, she stepped beside him. "It was nice to see you again, Eli."

Before he could respond, his phone dinged and lit up with a picture of a sleeping little girl sucking her thumb. Amara's stomach clenched at the thought of Eli's family. She hated to think of someone else claiming him. It had been years; her heart shouldn't bleed because he'd moved on. Amara's emotions were simply too close to the surface from the long night.

That was all.

Eli stepped into an elevator. "It was good to see you too. How long do you think it will be before it doesn't feel a little weird?"

Never.

Amara let out a soft chuckle to cover the nerves spinning through her stomach. "Did it feel weird?"

Eli raised an eyebrow and laughed with her. "Maybe just a bit."

"Yes," Amara agreed, enjoying the sound of Eli's laugh. The rich sound reverberated in the enclosed space, and she felt her shoulders relax. They could do this, work together and be friendly.

The spell broke as the elevator doors opened on the parking level. How was she supposed to do this? Amara forced a casual smile as Eli offered her a small wave before heading in the opposite direction.

"Goodbye," Amara whispered before pulling her keys from her purse. Tomorrow would be better. She'd be prepared to see him, and the raw emotions scorching her now would be dulled. She could do this—*she could.*

"Damn it!" Eli's curse echoed in the parking garage as she reached her car.

Her key was in her door; Amara could pretend she hadn't heard anything, but she hated the unkind thought. Her body was wired from being near him all night, but Amara blew out a breath. It shouldn't matter that Eli was her ex; he was a colleague who'd had a long night and wanted to get home to his family. If anyone else had sounded distressed, she wouldn't hesitate to see what was wrong.

Tossing her purse in the front seat, Amara locked her car and followed the sounds of Eli's rant to the other side of the parking garage. Her eyes widened as she watched him kick at the wheel clamp that had been placed on his left back tire. "Did you break any of your toes?"

"No!" Eli huffed as he leaned against the driver's side door. "I forgot to renew my parking pass."

"Parking security at Boston Gen. seems pretty serious. Don't most places just slap a ticket on your window?"

Eli glared at the bright yellow wheel clamp. "Our parking attendant takes her job very seriously." Eli pulled out his phone. "Fiona, I'm sorry about the pass. It slipped my mind with everything. Call me back, please." He blew out an exasperated breath as Amara leaned beside him. "She'll call back eventually. Guess if I want to go home sooner I need to order an Uber."

She jiggled her keys. "Want a lift?" Amara made the offer without thinking—but she couldn't withdraw it now. Forcing herself to sound cheery, she joked, "You have to promise not to kick my tires, though."

Eli's eyes wandered across her, and Amara held her breath. He used to be able to read her so easily. Did he realize how uneasy he made her? How part of her wished she'd just gotten in her car and gone home? *And* that an even larger part of Amara yearned to lean into Eli and pretend that a decade hadn't passed?

For almost three years, he'd been her sanctuary. The person she told her secrets and fears to. The world had disappeared when she was in Eli's arms. No other partner had ever managed to make her feel so loved and cherished.

Except their love hadn't been enough to make him put her first once the residency searches had begun. And his desire to be the best had colored every choice. Amara was a nurse. Of course she cared about her patients, but you had only one family. Once they were gone…

Water under the bridge, she reminded herself.

They'd been young and still expected the world to be kind when they'd found each other. The universe didn't operate on kindness or fairness. If it did, Boston Gen. wouldn't have such a hard time balancing its accounting books while serving its community. The sick would be able to get care regardless of their ability to pay, and her mother would have found a man to truly stand beside her in sickness and in health.

The air seemed to evaporate as she stared at Eli. He still hadn't answered her. Amara shrugged.

Fine. She wasn't going to beg him to let her drive him home. "Have a good day, Eli."

She hadn't taken three steps before he was striding next to her. "What if one of your tires looks at me weird?"

"What?" Amara stared at his brilliant grin.

"Am I allowed to kick one of your tires if it looks at me weird?" Eli winked. "Usually my jokes are funny, but I'm tired. I'll do better next time."

"Oh, my gosh, Eli Collins tells dad jokes, now." His grin sent a small thrill through her.

"I guess I do."

Just for a moment, Amara thought he might reach for her.

But of course he didn't.

Placing his hands in his pockets, Eli matched each of her strides. He'd done that years ago too. Slowing his gait to make sure they stayed together. Pressing her keys into her palms, Amara wanted to shake herself. She was looking for small things to hold on to, and that wasn't going to make working beside Eli any easier.

Eli sent a quick text to his mom, thanking her for the picture of Lizzy as he gave Amara directions to his home. His mom had told him to let her know if she sent too many pictures, but Eli couldn't get enough.

That still shocked him. Sam had always loved kids. He'd volunteered as a Big Brother to elementary school kids while in college and med school, and had developed a repertoire of dad jokes before he'd even met his wife. His brother had also gone into pediatric surgery.

But Eli hadn't felt drawn to kids, not like Sam. He'd done his pediatric rotations but never considered its specialties. The adrenaline of the ER was too great. He'd been so focused on his goals that he'd never thought of being a parent.

No, his mind ruthlessly reminded him. He'd thought about it. Specifically, how Amara would be a wonderful mother…

"Your daughter is adorable." Amara glanced at another image on his phone.

"Lizzy is my niece," Eli stated. He needed Amara to know that. It seemed ridiculous after all their time apart, but Eli wanted her to know he hadn't found someone else. She'd been right. Family was important. A lesson he hadn't fully learned until he'd taken Lizzy in. At least he hadn't ever seen the despair his mother had fi-

nally learned to hide hovering on his own partner's face.

Like it had clung to Amara so long ago.

"Sam and his wife died in a plane crash about
eight months ago, and Lizzy came to live with
me." His voice caught just a bit, as it always did
when he talked about Sam.

"I'm so sorry, Eli." Amara's hand reached for
his. She squeezed it once but then let go.

Clearing his throat, Eli clenched his fist to keep
from reaching for her hand. That simple touch
sent fire up his arm. He'd spent years dreaming
of her, and now she was here, so close, and there
was no reason for him to hold her hand. Or push
the lock of hair away from her cheek, ask what
she was thinking, kiss her... All those things
he'd taken for granted until she'd walked away.

Leaning back against the headrest, he
drummed his fingers against his knees. "I have
no experience with kids. Sam met Yolanda at a
pediatric surgical conference. The two were natural parents. I'm not really sure what I'm doing."

"I think most parents feel that way." Amara
shot him a quick wink. "For every parent that
rarely has doubts, I suspect there are hundreds
that question every minor decision."

"Do you have children?" She'd wanted to be a mother, a wife… Was her husband waiting for her at home? Was she going to send her kids off to school before climbing into bed?

"No." Amara's tone was light, but he saw her lip tremble. His eyes flashed to her bare ring finger, and she shook her head. "Not married."

He stared out the window. "I'm not married either." The words sounded so stilted, and Eli wanted to slap himself. Luckily, Amara seemed willing to let the statement go.

For years he'd been jealous of a man who didn't exist. The thought reverberated around his skull as the traffic inched forward. Eli had always figured Amara would find someone. A man to have a life with, to love. It hurt to think of her with someone else, but the slight wobble in her lip hurt more. She was alone, and there was more to the story, but he couldn't ask—*shouldn't*.

The car was silent as Amara stopped at a red light. They'd hit downtown at morning rush hour, and the gridlock stretched before them. It didn't matter that they were trying to go only a few miles, the red parking brakes highlighted the extended time they were going to spend together.

"How old is Lizzy?" Amara's question broke the uncomfortable silence.

"Almost two. I have to figure out how to throw a birthday party in a few months." Eli shook his head. What did you do for a two-year-old's birthday?

"Now, that is definitely one of those minor issues that you *don't* need to worry about." She let out a soft chuckle. "You just get a cake and a few presents. Parties aren't hard. I seem to remember throwing you a very cheap one my senior year."

"It wasn't cheap!" Eli protested. Amara had thrown him a surprise party in college. They'd played loud music, danced with friends and had a blast. It had been perfect—she'd been perfect.

"I hung streamers that I got seventy-five percent off because they'd lost half their dye sitting in the store's sunny window. I handed out chintzy dollar store hats. I only splurged on the magic relighting candles."

"I loved everything about that party." Eli smiled as she grinned at him. "Except for the relighting candles. We could have burned down the apartment with the way those things were sparking."

Amara shook her head. A few strands of her

dark hair had come loose from her braided bun, and she pushed them behind her ear and said, "No, we could not have!"

Eli laughed. "So, what kind of cake do you think I should get for Lizzy?" It wasn't one of the hundreds of questions he wanted to ask, but birthday parties seemed like a safe topic right now.

Much safer than *Have you thought about us for the last ten years too?*

"A pretty one. I bet the grocery store has a book you can pick from. Lizzy's so little that she won't remember the specifics. She'll just feel loved. That's what matters most, Eli," Amara said.

He shrugged. That sounded simple, but how did you convey love to a toddler? "I want her party to be special. To be the best!"

"No pressure." Amara playfully rolled her eyes. "It's a toddler's party. Does she like princesses? Or flowers or superheroes?"

"She enjoys *The Princess and the Frog* story. We read it at least ten times a week," Eli replied. Right after she'd come to live with him, he had painted her room bright yellow and hung pink flower carvings across it. It looked almost exactly like the room she'd had at her home. It was a small thing, but Lizzy had climbed into his lap for the first time that night and dropped *The Princess and the Frog* in his hand. That was the moment when Eli had felt like he might be able to handle fatherhood.

The weird feeling of parental pride and grief warred inside him. Sam should be the one planning the party, but he wasn't here. Shaking the thought away, Eli continued, "She likes dolls too. She carries around one that Mom got her. It's named Baby."

"Nothing like the creativity of young children." Amara's face lit up. "You could get her a doll cake. I always wanted one of those. One of the grocery stores had a display. The cake was the doll's dress, and she looked so pretty. I used to beg Mom to get me one, but she always made my cakes. That's another option. You could bake Lizzy's cake!" Amara's eyes sparkled with the dare.

He was a better cook now than he had been, but not by much. Before he took custody of Lizzy, most of his meals had come from the hospital vending machine or the frozen food aisle at the grocery store. Eli threw a hand over his heart. "I feel like you might be mocking my fear of birthday party planning."

Amara shook her head, but her lips twitched. "Maybe a little." She met his gaze and shrugged. "Or a lot."

The traffic finally started to clear, and Eli almost hated to see it move. He needed to get home, but the last thirty minutes had almost felt like old times. As he gave Amara directions to his place, part of him didn't want it to end.

A large part.

A car was sitting in Eli's short driveway. He frowned as Amara pulled in next to it. Any other morning he might have been excited that his father had finally stopped by. But Marshall's timing was terrible. He'd agreed to look at some of The Collins Research Group medical studies. Eli hoped reviewing the papers might help overcome the distance between them. Maybe then his father would see him as an equal. That would be almost as good as landing in the *US News & Reports* rankings.

Maybe better.

Still, it was too early to deal with his father. Amara was here. Marshall Collins could wait for a few minutes.

"Remember to pay for your parking pass, Dr. Collins."

Amara's grin chased away the worry pooling in Eli's stomach. "What if I want to use the excuse of not having a pass in order to see the new nurse at Boston Gen. after our shifts at the ER?" The question left his lips, and Eli's chest seized as he waited for her reaction.

Amara sucked in a breath, but she didn't tell him to knock it off. That was enough for him to take a risk. Eli wasn't ready to say goodbye. *Not again.*

"Want to meet Lizzy?" That was safer than asking if she might want to grab dinner or a drink.

Amara looked toward his town house before she shook her head. "I don't think that's a good idea."

"Why not?" The question was out before he had time to think. He wasn't sure he wanted whatever answer Amara was going to give.

She offered Eli a tired smile. "We…it's been a long time…" Amara shrugged.

It had been a long time. Too long.

A sharp knock interrupted them, and Amara jumped.

Marshall Collins motioned for Amara to roll down her window. Before Eli could stop her, she did. Why hadn't his father waited for Eli to come inside? Better yet, why hadn't he called or texted, like he usually did?

"The Collins Research Group made some headway on the study you recommended. There are some papers I want you to look over." Marshall looked past Amara. He hadn't bothered to say hello to his son either, but the slight against Amara annoyed Eli more.

"Good morning, Marshall." He'd stopped referring to his father by anything else after their argument over Eli's refusal to go into surgery. Not that it seemed to bother Marshall. "You remember Amara Patel."

"Good morning." Amara yawned.

"I need you to look over this research, Eli," Marshall repeated, handing him a stack of papers through the window and then heading toward his car.

"Still not big on small talk, huh?" Amara remarked as Marshall got into his vehicle and drove away. Gesturing to the stack of papers, Amara asked, "You help at The Collins Research Group?"

"I work for the company part-time and serve on the board." Eli flipped through the documents.

"When do you sleep?" Amara stared at him, but the playful exchange they'd had a moment before had evaporated with Marshall's appearance.

Eli shrugged. "I get by. Want to come inside? I have tea."

Amara's nose scrunched up as she stared at him. "I seem to remember you saying that tea was the worst caffeine infusion there was." Her eyes dipped to the papers in his lap, and her small smile disappeared again.

"I don't drink the stuff." Eli rubbed his forehead, trying to determine how much to say. She was so close, and he didn't want her to leave or to scare her away. "The cupboard never looked right without a can of tea next to the coffee." So much hadn't looked right, felt right, without the little touches Amara added to his life.

"Eli." Amara's fingers grazed his leg, and she bit her lip as she yanked them back. "We can't do this."

Heat traveled across his body where Amara's

fingers had touched him. His heart beat faster as her eyes held his.

Stay with me.

Eli kept those words buried deep inside as she leaned back. "It's just tea."

"Is it?" Her eyes once more darted to the stack of papers in his lap.

No!

Before he could find any words, Amara continued, "I need to get going. Get some rest, Eli." She started the car. "See you at the hospital."

"Thank you for the ride." He got out and watched her drive away before heading into the house. His body was heavy with exhaustion, but the light of hope was burning in his heart. Amara was at Boston Gen.

CHAPTER THREE

AMARA'S STOMACH RUMBLED as she headed to room 4. She made sure to keep her head down as she passed Eli. During the last two shifts, she'd kept her distance. When they were working on a patient, Amara made sure to leave as soon as the job was done. No more personal conversations in the doorway after difficult cases. No time alone. She was at Boston General to work, not to reconnect with Eli.

She wasn't the same person anymore. *Inside or out.* Life had scarred her in more ways than she'd thought possible as the happy nursing student who'd dated Eli.

He was a different person too. And for a moment—a long moment—she'd wanted to go into his home, meet Lizzy and enjoy that cup of tea. Find out if the connection between them had survived both time and distance. But then she'd stared at the stack of papers in Eli's lap and pushed that desire aside.

Even if she was interested, which she wasn't, where would she fit into his life now? Eli was working part-time for Marshall, on the board at The Collins Research Group, and maintaining a full schedule at Boston Gen. And he was raising Lizzy.

A smile touched her lips as she thought about Eli as a father. He'd be a great dad, *was* a great dad. Bad fathers didn't worry about birthday cakes. Amara wasn't sure her father could recite her date of birth without checking his calendar. Any extra time Eli managed to carve out of his intense calendar would go to Lizzy.

As it should.

The sob echoing from room 4 surprised Amara. The triage nurse had stated the patient likely needed a few stitches, but it was marked as a minor issue. As she opened the door, another racking sob traveled down the hall, and she saw Eli start toward the room.

Why couldn't one of the other doctors have been close by?

Amara shook herself at the selfish thought. Eli was one of the finest emergency room doctors she'd worked with. If this patient was experiencing something more than what the triage nurse had identified, then he was the best one to see to it. The patient mattered more than her fragile heart.

A young woman with a bandage on her cheek was bawling on the bed. She didn't look up as Amara and Eli stepped into the room.

Quickly washing her hands and donning gloves, Amara sat carefully on the edge of the bed. "I'm Amara. What's your name?" she asked, her voice soft but firm.

"Han… Ha… Hannah," she sobbed.

"I'm Dr. Collins," Eli stated as he put on a pair of gloves. "What's going on?"

"I cut my cheek!" Hannah cried as she stared at them.

Amara nodded and raised her hands. "Can I take a look?" Blood coated Hannah's cheek, but the wound wasn't bleeding through the bandage. Amara gently pulled aside the dressing, revealing a long cut from the side of Hannah's nose to just under the edge of her right eye.

The wound was going to need several stitches, but Amara was surprised by Hannah's reaction. Some patients didn't handle pain well, but Amara didn't think that was the issue. Scars were frightening, *life-changing* sometimes, and there would always be a hint of one on Hannah's cheek. Taking a guess, she stated, "The scar won't be that bad."

"Yes, it will." The girl's watery stare met hers. "I tripped over the bathroom mat, hit the counter, and now I'll have this large ugly scar forever." Hannah's wail echoed in the small room. "And then Brandon will break up with me."

Amara's heart broke at the sad statement. She wanted to reassure Hannah that her fear was impossible. *But...*

"You are a lovely young woman." Eli's voice was calm and so sure as he tilted Hannah's head to get a better look at the wound. "No one is going to dump you for a scar, which will soon be barely noticeable. Right, Amara?"

Her throat seized as she looked between Hannah and Eli, but she managed to nod before heading to grab the suture supplies Eli would need. That hadn't been her own experience. But the scars on her body were much more significant than a cut across the cheek.

Joe had said her independence, her refusal to rely on him for everything—anything—had caused their breakup. But he hadn't looked at her the same way after her surgery. Joe was never able to see past the ragged scars on her chest.

So it was a good thing she hadn't relied on him.

She'd hoped it was just Joe. But the few men she'd dated since had ghosted her after she'd told them what she'd been through, despite telling her it wasn't an issue.

Get it together, Amara mentally chastised herself.

She threaded the needle as Eli numbed Hannah's cheek.

"And *if* someone can't see past a scar, then that means there's a problem with them, not you," Eli stated. His voice was low and comforting, and Amara saw Hannah take a deep breath.

Eli was an excellent doctor, and Amara was glad that he'd been the one to follow her into Hannah's room. Amara handed him the needle and saw him look to her.

"A problem with them," Eli repeated, holding her gaze for just a moment.

Her breath caught, but she nodded before returning her focus to Hannah. Eli's statement was so sure, so confident. He wouldn't see a minor scar as an issue, but Amara's weren't minor…

She patted Hannah's hand. "You are beautiful. Imperfections are what make us special." Her tone was upbeat, peppy, but uncertainty pressed against her spine.

"Your belly is rumbling," Hannah stated as she wiped away a tear from her uninjured cheek.

Amara winked, glad that their patient was focusing on something other than the row of stitches Eli was putting in her cheek. "Yes, well, nurses don't always get lunch breaks."

"Don't you worry about Amara," Eli told his patient as he tied a final stitch. "I'll make sure she gets a break as soon as we're done here."

The small bursts of excitement popping through her body when she was near Eli shouldn't be happening. Amara knew that, but for a moment she didn't care. He'd been so sincere when he told Hannah her scar wouldn't matter—and it wouldn't. But he'd managed to take away just a bit of the pain Amara carried with her, as well. What would he think if he knew that her scars wouldn't disappear, would always make her body look different?

Not that it mattered, because Amara wasn't going to mention them.

She wasn't.

* * *

Amara had avoided him over their last few shifts. Eli tried to ignore the pain that pierced him each time she averted her eyes. They were colleagues now. That knowledge did nothing to stop the ache in his heart.

"Your stomach isn't rumbling, it's growling. And mine is turning over on itself," Eli said as they exited Hannah's room. "The ER is…" Eli looked around and pursed his lips. Saying an ER was quiet was almost guaranteed to result in a wave of patients.

"You almost jinxed us." Amara's lips tipped up into a smile, and his heart untwisted just a bit.

"But I didn't!" Eli nodded toward the staff lounge. "Let's take our break. Eat when you can—right?"

Amara's eyes shifted to the door, and he could see her hesitate.

Her belly growled again, and Amara glared at it before laughing. "Sounds like my stomach is answering in the affirmative."

She pulled a small lunch box from her locker and sat at the small table in the corner while Eli headed for the vending machine.

He wouldn't push, but something about Hannah's scar had affected Amara. She hadn't had any significant scars when he'd known her, but she had them now. He was almost certain. And someone had made her think they made her less than perfect.

"Hannah's scar won't be that bad," Eli stated as he fed a dollar into the machine. "Scars fade over time." Amara didn't say anything, but he saw her frown as she poured some dressing on her salad.

Her eyebrows rose as he tossed a chocolate bar, bag of chips and a granola bar on the table. "That is not a meal."

Eli shrugged. "My mother says the same thing, but it's easy."

Amara looked at her wilted salad and glared at it. "Mine is almost as sad, but at least there are nutrients in it."

Her knee bumped his under the table, and he saw her bite her lip. Was being close to him making her think about them too?

"How is your mother?" Amara asked as she pulled her knees to the side.

Eli swallowed as heat ran along his neck. He was craving tiny touches, bumped shoulders, knees, any contact as long as it was from Amara.

If Eli was smart, he'd avoid her. He still wanted to be the best doctor, still thought the hospital and the patients were the most important thing. But he was balancing family life now, and doing it well, in his opinion.

But could he tell Amara she came first? *No*, his brain counseled as his heart cried *yes*. Still, the thought of not spending any time with her hurt more than the moments where she pulled away.

"Mom is doing well. She loves being a grandma. Lizzy calls her Oma. I have a room set up for her at the town house where she stays when I'm on night shift. Mom started taking watercolor classes a few years ago. Her studio puts on an art show each session. I always make sure to request the night off so Lizzy and I can cheer her on."

"You take nights off for an art show?" Amara's eyes were wide, and she shook her head. "That is sweet. I bet your mother loves it." Her voice died away as she pushed her salad around with her fork.

She was surprised he'd take a night off work. "Of course." Eli kept his voice level, but defensiveness flooded him.

Letting out a deep breath, Eli pointed to a flyer

on the corkboard. "Her next show is at the end of next week at the community center on Ridge Avenue. Since I'm on day shift then, I can go after work. Susan stops by sometimes. Mom loves showing off."

"I'm on day shift next week too." Amara dabbed her lips with a napkin. "I'd…"

The door to the lounge opened, interrupting whatever Amara planned to say. Dr. Griffin Stanfred's eyes hovered on them for a moment. "There you two are." Griffin called as he walked toward them.

Eli saw Amara's shoulders tense, and she started packing up her food without looking at him. They were just eating. Why was she acting like they'd been caught doing something wrong?

"I need to get back to the nurses' station," Amara stated as she pushed back from the table.

"Bye, Amara," Eli called as she headed for the door.

Griffin raised an eyebrow as he sat in Amara's recently vacated seat. "Did you two fight?"

"Why would you say that?" Eli shook his head. Long hours in the hospital often resulted in hospital staff dating, and he'd seen a few epic arguments after bad breakups. But they'd been eating in the lounge not…

I needed a change…

Amara's words from the other night cascaded across Eli's memory.

Was that why she was here?

Griffin's playful joke hadn't meant anything, but rumors had been started on less. Eli sighed as Griffin launched into a recital of plans for Boston Gen. It was usually Eli's favorite topic, but he couldn't seem to focus on the conversation tonight.

Amara grinned as sunshine hit her cheeks. After a week of night shifts, she was enjoying seeing the sun instead of the moon. She'd decided to try the food truck parked outside the hospital. Anything was better than the salad she'd eaten the other night with Eli.

She was glad Griffin had interrupted them. Amara had been about to say that she'd love to see his mother's art show. That was too close to asking Eli on a date. And she did not want to admit to herself how much she might want that.

Might…

Spending time with Eli felt good. That was a

dangerous thought, but Amara couldn't push it away. The brief snatches of time they'd had sitting in her car, talking in the hall, had sent her heart racing. It was terrifying, but Amara was finding it harder to come up with reasons to keep her distance. Or maybe she just didn't care to look for reasons…

"The tacos are the best thing they make." Eli stated as Amara looked up from the food truck's menu. "Honestly, you will not be sorry if you get two of them and then come sit in the courtyard with me."

Amara returned Eli's smile and tried to ignore the energy that danced along her skin anytime he was nearby. After she'd fled the other night, he hadn't pushed her for reasons why. Eli had just kept smiling and asked how she was over their next few shifts. It was such a small thing, but Amara couldn't stop herself from looking forward to seeing him each day.

"Two tacos, please." Amara handed over her money before looking at Eli again. "I'm trusting you."

But only with tacos, Amara reminded herself. If she got close to him again, and it didn't work out… Amara's throat felt tight as fear wrapped around her. She never wanted to feel that much heartache again.

Eli placed a hand over his heart and took a playful bow. "They're great; I promise." Lifting the lid of his own container, he continued, "See, tacos."

Amara laughed as she stared at the foil-wrapped food. "You realize right now they just look like tinfoil. You could have anything in there."

"But they're tacos," he said. *"Promise."* Amara thanked the worker as the tacos were handed to her. The food did smell almost divine. She started to walk back toward the hospital but stopped. Eli had invited her to sit with him. Could she just walk over and sit down?

Should she?

Taking a deep breath, Amara stood in the warm sun, fighting her indecision. It was just a friendly lunch between colleagues. Except they weren't just colleagues. They were exes, and she'd left Massachusetts Research after a breakup. Most hospital romances didn't work out.

Most romances anywhere.

She knew that, but her feet seemed to move of their own accord.

Eli grinned as she took the seat across from him. If he'd noticed her hesitation, he didn't say so. Instead, he just handed her a few paper napkins. "I forgot to mention that the tacos get messy."

"Thanks for the warning." His fingers brushed hers, and Amara forced herself to keep breathing as heat and desire raced along her body. She knew Eli had an effect on most women. The man was the definition of temptation. He was absolutely gorgeous, intelligent and charming. But Amara felt like their connection had been unique. Stronger, almost ordained by the universe. It was a ridiculous notion, but Amara had never been able to fully shake it. And she'd never felt it with anyone else.

"How is Lizzy?" The little girl was a safe topic. Plus she loved seeing Eli talk about his niece. He glowed—it was adorable.

"Ornery, but all the books I've read say that's normal for toddlers." Eli pulled up his phone and opened his camera. It was full of images of Lizzy, and Amara's heart wanted to explode at the cuteness. "She was getting into everything last night. I think I waited too long to babyproof the place."

Amara laughed at a picture of her wearing a pot on her head. "Did you give Lizzy the pot to play with? Or did she pull it out of the cupboard?"

Eli sighed and pulled up another picture. "It was a mutual decision that she would play with the pots while I ensured she was unable to get to the cleaning products or open the fridge."

His eyes softened as he showed her another photo. "She was still toddling around when she came to live with me eight months ago. I swear she learned to run overnight."

Amara laughed, "My mother always liked to say *It was just yesterday that you were two.* I hated it as a teenager and thought she was crazy. How could sixteen years just fly by? I get it now. Time seems to speed up the older we get."

Eli nodded. "I know. I blinked, and a decade went by."

Amara looked at him.

Was he talking about them?

Did it matter?

Amara had spent more time thinking about Eli over the last week than her brain wanted to admit. Her heart wanted Amara to remember all the fun times they'd shared. And there had been so many good moments. She swallowed the last bite of her taco and pushed back from the table. "Thanks for the recommendation. I need to get back inside."

"If I'm free and the weather is nice, this is my standard break spot. You're welcome anytime."

Amara nodded and started to get up. She wasn't running...she wasn't.

"Oh, one more thing." Eli tapped her shoulder. Her heart leaped.

Was Eli going to ask her out?

She'd say no. Of course, she'd say no. "What?" Amara was stunned by how level her voice was.

"Their tacos are amazing." Eli closed his own box and dumped them both in the trash. Leaning over, he whispered, "But their club sandwich is the worst. Seriously, you will regret spending six dollars on it—it's terrible."

He was so close, if she turned her head at all, her lips would graze his cheek. That thought sent desire racing through her. "Good to know." Amara breathed out.

Then he winked and walked away.

Amara's heart skipped several beats as she watched Eli head into the hospital. He hadn't even waited to walk in with her. She'd completely misread the situation.

Which was good, she thought, trying to rationalize away the little bit of hurt she felt. That way, she didn't have to tell him no. Because she would have.

Shaking her head, Amara headed back into the hospital. She did not want to examine the discomfort in her stomach or the tightness in her chest. She was fine.

She was.

Amara waved as she stepped up to the food truck, and Eli felt his insides dance. He still hadn't managed to work up the courage to ask her out. In fact, he'd practically run away the first time they'd eaten together. Afraid his question would bubble out before he was ready. But he looked forward to meeting her at the truck. She'd joined him each day for lunch. That had to mean something, right?

That she wants to be friends? his mind ruthlessly asked. Even though his brain raced with thoughts of what if, that didn't mean hers did. Eli forced those thoughts away.

"They were out of tacos!" Amara complained

as she opened her container displaying, a sad-looking sandwich.

"Tell me you didn't order the club sandwich after I warned you." Eli gripped her hand and then immediately let it go. It was so easy to be around Amara, and yet so hard. Reaching for her had been unintentional, but he wanted to do it again. Pull her close and just hold her.

Amara's eyes shifted to his hand, and Eli swallowed the nervousness crawling through him. He forced himself to look at the sorry bread lying in Amara's container. "It's the club, isn't it?"

"No!" Amara's hand tapped his arm, and then she placed both her hands on the table. Was she afraid touching him would lead to wanting more too?

"It's a BLT. It does look rather sad, doesn't it?" She sighed.

"Switch with me." Eli offered his tacos. "I only took one bite. They're still perfectly good."

"I can't take your tacos." Amara stared at them, eyeing the unopened tinfoil. "At least not the one you already took a bite of."

He laughed as she traded him half her sandwich.

How had he ever let her walk away?

"Want to get dinner somewhere better than this?" The question hovered between them, and Eli's insides tossed as she looked away. He wanted her to say yes, *needed it*.

"I—I—I'm not sure," Amara stuttered.

Eli held up his hand. "No problem, Amara. I can wait."

"You can?" Her brown eyes glittered as she looked at him. "I don't know if…" Amara broke off and shook her head. "I'm not the same person."

"I'm not either." Eli shrugged. "Maybe that means…" He blew out a breath. "I like spending time with you." That was the truth, all of it. For the last week, he'd gone to bed each night thinking of her, woken each morning thinking of her. She'd wormed her way into his heart years ago, and he'd never gotten over her.

Never even tried…

Eli pushed the thought away and held up the awful looking sandwich. It looked remarkably unappetizing. Leaning forward, he whispered, "If they're out of tacos, order the chicken salad."

Amara rolled her eyes "Now you tell me."

Amara pulled at the edge of her skirt and tried to work up the courage to open her car door. Or turn the ignition back on and head home. She wasn't even sure why she'd decided to come to Eli's mother's art show. Sitting at home alone watching television hadn't held much appeal, even though it was her standard Friday evening routine.

So she'd come here... Eli had said Susan usually came, and the head nurse had told Amara she might stop by. It *was* just an art show, and she wanted to support Martha. That was all.

Sucking in a deep breath, Amara counted to three and then forced herself to open the door. She'd driven all the way here, and Martha had been kind to her in the past. Amara could do this.

Besides, Eli would be busy with his mother and Lizzy. He wouldn't have time to spend with her. She was just here to see the watercolors. The argument sounded so weak her heart laughed at her.

"Amara?"

Eli's voice caught her off guard, and she gripped the side of the car to keep from tumbling over.

"I didn't mean to startle you," Eli stated as he stepped closer. "I was just leaving and—"

"Is the show over?" Amara interrupted. She'd

thought the flyer said it went until nine, and she hadn't been in her car that long.

Eli smiled and shook his head. "No, it's just getting going. But Mom isn't feeling well. I came to let her instructor know she wouldn't be able to make it."

"Oh." What was she supposed to say? "Well…" Amara brain fumbled for something to say as she stared at Eli. He was dressed in dark gray pants and a light blue button-up that accented his dark eyes. He looked delectable and dangerous and like all the things she wanted.

Why had she thought coming here was a good idea?

"I didn't get a chance to walk around, and I already hired a babysitter. Want to take a gander?" Eli's eyes never left hers as he offered his arm. How was it fair for any man to look this good?

She *was* already here. "Sure." Her heart shuddered as she slipped her arm through his. This was a mistake; she knew it, but Amara suddenly didn't care. It was one art show, one night, nothing more. "Make sure you point out which ones are your mom's."

Eli opened the door to the community center. "Just try to stop me."

* * *

If there had been a slow-motion camera on him when Eli saw Amara get out of her car, he knew it would have showed him picking his jaw up off the ground.

He'd blinked a few times before he'd believed it was really her. The black skirt she wore hugged her hips perfectly, and the flowy pink top she had on made his mouth water. Amara's dark hair was wrapped in an intricate bun, and Eli could barely keep his mind from wandering past the thoughts of what it might look like down, and remembering how it felt as he ran his fingers through it.

"Isn't this lovely?" Amara stared at the picture of a bowl of fruit sitting right in front of the door.

"That's the image many of the novice students worked from," Eli whispered. "You'll see it recreated a lot in here." He had helped his mother hang her work last night and had already seen all the paintings currently on display. But if Amara was here, nothing was going to drag him away.

"Oh." Amara's fingers brushed her lips. "So where are your mom's paintings, then?"

Amara had dropped her hold on Eli's arm as

soon as they stepped through the front door. His arm felt painfully bare without it.

Gesturing toward the back, he guided her through the crowded facility. Eli was grateful for the small excuses to touch her. The moments were fleeting, but they were all he had.

"This is Mom's bowl of fruit." Eli couldn't stop himself from sounding proud. He knew his mother's work was amateur, but she'd come so far over the last few years. "You can see that she uses light more, and her strokes are finer."

Amara smiled at him and shook her head. "Sorry, Eli. I have no idea what I'm looking at. I mean, I know it's a bowl of fruit. A very nice bowl of fruit, and it looks so…" Amara's eyes widened as she caught herself.

She looked at the people passing them and leaned toward him. "Hers look better than the ones at the front, but I don't see the brush-strokes."

Her lips were centimeters from his cheek, and he was thrilled she'd wanted to quietly mention how much better his mom's paintings were. It was silly and kind and exactly the sort of thing Eli expected from Amara. The fact that it also meant she was so close to him was a delightful bonus.

Closing the distance slightly, Eli whispered, "I'm happy to show you whatever you like."

Her smile sent a shiver of longing through him. Eli forced himself to turn toward the paintings before he gave in to the urge to kiss her. He'd promised her time, and Eli could be patient.

He could.

Eli's throat felt dry, but he managed to outline what his mother had told him about the paintings. Somehow, forcing words past the desire clouding his mind.

It was lovely watching Eli gush over his mother's paintings. They were good, not gallery quality, but his mother had skill. And Eli's pride in her accomplishments sent such a wave of emotion through her that Amara didn't think she'd stopped smiling since she got here. Thank goodness she'd gotten out of her car.

"Thanks for staying with me, Eli." Amara's skin was hot despite stepping into the cool night air after the show. This hadn't been a date, but she'd enjoyed spending time with him.

"Thank you for coming. Mom will be so glad you made it." His deep voice carried in the empty parking lot.

Where had the time gone?

"Tell Martha her paintings were beautiful." Amara held her car door to keep from touching Eli, again. If she did, she'd kiss him. And he'd kiss her back. That knowledge made her grip the door even harder.

"I will. She'll be sorry to have missed you." Eli's gaze held hers, but he didn't lean toward her.

Her decision would be so much easier if he did. But Eli stood still, just staring at Amara. Making her want all the things she was trying to convince herself she didn't need.

"I should get going." The words were breathless. Should she hug him? No, that would lead to kisses too. And Amara would lose the final bit of control she was clinging onto.

Eli placed his hands in his pockets and tipped his head. "Good night, Amara." The bubble of tension between them burst as he walked away.

She ran her fingers along her unkissed lips as her body trembled with emotion. She'd made the right choice. She had… Kisses would lead to her wanting more, and Amara already wanted more than was good for her.

CHAPTER FOUR

"HERBAL TEA." ELI smiled as he handed it over.

The deep dimple in his cheek sent a thrill through Amara as she took the cup from his hand. His thumb brushed her pinky, and she couldn't ignore the butterflies that floated through her belly. Eli had delivered a cup of herbal tea to her during her last three shifts.

"Thanks." Amara put the warm cup between her fingers.

Do you wish I'd kissed you the other night? She bit back the question.

He hadn't asked her out again, and there weren't any more art shows that she could crash anytime soon. That should make her happy, but it didn't.

He was different now, her heart argued. Eli took off shifts for art shows, went home on time. He video-called Lizzy at bedtime if the hospital wasn't swamped. And Amara could fall for him again. If she let herself…

She looked for him when she was on shift. The last two days, she'd even arrived a few minutes early just to be able to catch him in the staff lounge before their work started. If she wanted to protect her heart, Amara needed to stop.

But Eli made her laugh. Something she hadn't done much after her mother died. And even less since Joe left her. Eli made her happy, and that felt dangerous. The walls she'd put around her heart a decade ago had protected her when other men walked away. But were they strong enough to protect her from Eli?

Nick, a radiology tech, rushed to the desk and laid a few images on the counter. "Can you see to the woman in room 10? Broken scaphoid." Then he was gone.

"Shall we go plaster a wrist?" Eli asked as she stood up and followed him into room 10 where an older woman was on her phone.

"Gotta go, Marie. A hot doctor and a smoking nurse just walked in to patch my busted hand. Should be able to make it to hang gliding next week."

"No, you won't." Eli shook his head. "You broke your wrist, ma'am."

"I know that, *young man.*" The patient was

wearing a jumpsuit and looked to be in good spirits as she winked at Amara. "Is he always this serious?"

"No." Amara bent her head, trying to keep the giggles at bay as she stepped beside the woman who had to be at least seventy. "How did you injure yourself?" Amara asked as she prepped the plaster for the cast.

"Call me, Dot, please." Their patient leaned on her uninjured hand as she studied Amara. "I broke it after skydiving."

"After?" Eli raised an eyebrow as he began to splint Dot's wrist.

"Yes, *after.*" Pushing a wisp of white hair behind her ear, Dot sighed. "I tripped over the step on the way to the car and tried to catch myself. Gone my whole life and never broken a bone. Seems like a shame to break the streak at seventy-five." Dot glared at the offending wrist. "It's not going to slow me down, though!"

Amara saw Eli look at her, but she didn't meet his gaze. If she looked at him, she was going to laugh. And Dot didn't need any encouragement!

"I'm sorry, but a broken wrist is going to slow you—at least a bit. You can't hang glide with a cast." Eli kept his tone firm, but Amara saw his lip twitch. He was impressed by Dot's spirit too.

"You sweet man, they strap you in with a partner. He'll be doing all the work—as he should." Dot's eyes twinkled as she smiled at Amara.

Eli didn't comment on Dot's joke, but Amara knew it took all his control. No doubt, he'd spend the rest of their shift regaling people with the story. "I'm impressed you're so active."

"Because I'm old?" Dot laughed as crimson stained Eli's cheeks. "No shame in admitting the truth. I spent the first sixty years of my life being careful. Do you know what it got me?" Her bottom lip quivered just a bit as she looked over Eli's shoulder.

"Nothing." Her large green eyes met Amara's. "It got me nothing. I never risked my heart or did anything that would result in broken bones. I hit retirement and realized I was alone with little to show for my sixty-plus years on this planet." Dot sighed.

An older gentleman stepped into the room, carrying two bottles of water. "They said no frozen margaritas in the ER, Dot."

"You tried bringing frozen margaritas into a hospital?" Eli said as he stared at the visitor.

"Of course not," he replied with such exaggerated vowels that Amara didn't know if he was kidding.

"This is Richard. My fiancé." Dot grinned as she gestured to her cast. "We're getting married in three weeks, and I'm going to have a purple cast."

"I'll just wear a purple tie to match." Richard laughed. "Does this mean we aren't skydiving on the honeymoon?"

"No!"

"Yes!"

Amara laughed as Dot and Eli answered at the same time. Then realization struck her. She wasn't risking anything either.

She wanted to scream as a chill raced down her back. She was letting fear rule her. Worrying that if she loved anyone too much, she'd get hurt, just like her mother. But fear hadn't gotten her anything either.

"We'll just have to find other ways to occupy our time." Dot laughed as Eli's face heated again. "Nice work, Doc." The woman twisted her wrist, admiring her cast. "It makes a real statement."

Amara stared at Eli. What if she let go of fear? Her heart wanted Eli, but what if... She shook her head. She'd lived a life of what-ifs, and she was still alone.

As Eli explained cast care to Dot, Amara slipped from the room and tried to gather her thoughts. Unfortunately, they were all over the place.

"Amara?" She turned as Eli spoke from behind her.

"Amara, Eli." Susan stated as she stepped between them.

Amara was grateful for the interruption and made sure to keep her gaze focused on Susan. But she could feel Eli's eyes on her.

"I wanted to let you know that you're partners for the health fair." Susan looked at Amara quickly before addressing Eli. "As last year's winner, you have the first pick of the booths, Dr. Collins."

"You won last year?"

Eli's eyes studied her, but he let the change of conversation happen. "I've won the last five years. And I'll win this year too. We'll win—I mean."

It took all her control not to sigh at the intensity in his eyes. "Seriously, Eli? It's only a community health fair."

"That helps Boston Gen. as well as the community. It makes people think of us. Community involvement should help us if we can figure out how to get on the survey for the national rankings. This year I'm even trying to get the press to show up. Our booth needs to be spectacular."

The national rankings...

Amara did sigh then. What was so important about a magazine that most people never read? She knew the list hit the major news sites, but it was splashed across the front page for only a few hours before dropping into the void of the internet for another year.

The nerve at the base of Eli's jaw twitched, and Amara took his hand. Under the sheen of self-assuredness, Eli doubted himself.

He was a remarkable doctor at a respected hospital—no matter what any piece of paper said. She squeezed his hand before dropping it quickly as she remembered herself. They were at work *and not together*, she reminded herself.

"Whatever we do will be great. I'm sure."

Eli nodded and looked across at Dot's room. "What happened in there? You suddenly looked..."

Another nurse passed Amara a chart, and she

looked it over rather than meet Eli's gaze. "Just a busy night, Eli. I'm fine."

"Not sure I believe that. I'm here if you want to talk." He blew out a breath.

Her mind flashed to the long conversations they used to share. And to the intimacy that had so often followed when their talking turned to touches and kisses. Her body heated, and she bit her lip. She needed to focus. Gripping the file, she offered him a polite smile. "I need to see to the patient in room 6. Thanks for the tea, Eli."

Glancing at the chart again, Amara frowned. The admitting nurse had only written *low-grade fever.* The patient had been sitting in the waiting room for a good part of the day. Most people would have gone home to wait out the infection, but Amara had treated many nonemergency issues during her years in the ER. Some people just worried.

As she walked into room 6, Amara nodded to the man sitting in the bed and he lowered his novel. He wore a paper mask over his face, and exhaustion coated his eyes. A bag of books and puzzle magazines sat on the end of the bed. He'd come prepared for a long wait.

"Good evening, Mr. Dyer. I'm Amara."

"Please call me Seth." His voice was hoarse. "Sorry for not shaking your hand, but my immune system is still compromised. Germs and chemo don't mix, I guess."

Amara almost lost her grip on the paper in front of her. "You're a cancer patient?"

Seth nodded. "Leukemia. Finished my second round of chemo last month."

She felt her stomach drop. Cancer had changed everything in Amara's life. Her grandmother had died when she was five, and her mother had lost her own battle with the disease three years ago. Neither woman had lived to see their fifty-fifth birthday. Then Amara lost part of herself in a quest to keep the dreaded disease from claiming her too.

When her mother's oncologist recommended Amara take the genetic test due to her grandmother's and mother's early-life diagnoses, she'd done it. And it had confirmed her fears. Amara's genes carried the BRAC1 marker, raising her risk for breast cancer to over 70 percent.

Amara had scheduled a preventative mastectomy the week after she'd received her results. But she'd been surprised how much she'd mourned the loss of her breasts. She was a nurse. She understood her risks, what the procedure entailed. Amara thought she'd prepared herself enough.

It had been a shock to realize that part of her was really gone forever. It was the right choice— she was certain of that. But it had taken Amara months to be able to fully examine her own scars. She still kept her eyes away from the mirror when she toweled off after a shower.

Joe hadn't touched her chest after the procedure, not even once. Everyone Amara had dated after looked at her differently when they found out. Then they stopped calling or texting. At least she knew why she was being ghosted. But that only encouraged the fear that never seemed to stop worming its way through her.

"You sat in the emergency room waiting area all day?" Amara wanted to scream at the admitting officials. Boston Gen. saw more trauma than most area hospitals, but a fever wasn't just a minor thing when you had a compromised immune system. He *should* have been back here hours ago and either treated and released or admitted.

"A car accident arrived right before I did. The

triage nurse was understandably busy. I wore my mask and isolated myself."

She'd seen other patients like this. People who didn't want to burden others with their condition and didn't want to admit they'd slipped from healthy to sick.

Rather than give Seth a lecture, she plastered on a smile. "Who's your oncologist, Seth?"

He fidgeted with the edge of his book. "My wife, kids and I are here from Florida visiting her parents. My oncologist, Dr. Peppertree, cleared the travel. But I think maybe I overdid it." Seth closed his eyes. "Still not used to treating my body with kid gloves."

She heard the frustration in his voice. Her mother had hated taking it easy too. She'd fought for every normal moment she could get.

Grabbing a thermometer, Amara ran it over Seth's forehead and behind his ear. His fever had risen, but only slightly. "You still have a fever. How are you feeling otherwise? I need all the symptoms, no matter how minor you think they might be."

"Tired, but I'm always tired. My throat is sore. Other than that, I just feel weak, like I have for the last six months. My boys are six and eleven. I used to play outside with them all the time. They walked the Freedom Trail today. My wife sent pictures, but…" Seth's voice cracked. "Sorry."

"You don't need to apologize." Grief warred within Amara, but Seth wasn't her mother. His cancer had a high survivability rate. If she let her emotions control her, she wouldn't be able to do her job. "Can you please write down the number for your oncologist? I am going to get a doctor and see if we can expedite your stay." She handed him a pen and a pad of paper.

Amara hustled down the hall and collided with Eli. His fingers gripped her shoulders for just a moment too long. The connection between them had always been electric, but now it burned. "I need you to see my patient in room 6," she told him.

"Can't. Four kids got into a knife fight on Salem Avenue. Multiple victims are arriving in the bay. You're with me," Eli stated as he moved down the hall.

"Eli!" Amara held her ground. "Seth's a cancer patient from out of town. He's got a fever, *and* he's been sitting in our waiting room all day!"

Eli shook his head, and she thought she heard

a curse slip from his lips. "We need to focus on the critical patient."

"I know, but…" Amara looked at the closed door where Seth had waited nearly all day to be seen.

Eli's eyes softened. His voice was low as he stared at her. "You know how triage works. I've got to see the kid that might bleed out *now*."

He was right, but that didn't stop Amara's feelings of failure as she followed him down the hall. Seth wasn't her mother—*he wasn't*. As soon as this crisis was over, she'd make sure he was taken care of. That was all she could do.

Seth had strep throat. Amara had delivered the lab work herself and then promptly taken off. Eli couldn't blame her. Today's shift had been terrible. They'd lost two of the stab wound patients. But Amara's reaction to the cancer patient had surprised Eli—something else was going on there, but he didn't know what.

Glancing at the clock, he sighed. They'd been off duty for twenty minutes. Eli had stayed to deliver the bad news to Seth that he'd have to be admitted until his infection cleared. Amara had already gone home. He needed to do the same.

As the elevator doors opened to the parking garage, Eli paused. Amara's car was still parked two cars away from his. He'd noticed where she'd parked ever since she'd given him a lift that first day. Eli wanted to pretend that the lot wasn't that big, so it was easy to notice her car. But it was a lie. He'd worked with Susan since his residency ended and couldn't pick out her vehicle. It was just Amara.

A soft sob echoed from her car as Eli passed by. If you worked in the ER, you left exhausted, tired and sad more days than most wanted to admit. No one should cry alone in a parking garage.

Eli stepped beside the passenger door and knocked. "Want some company?" Amara shrugged but didn't order him away. Climbing into the car, he reached for her hand. At least she wasn't alone now.

"Today sucked," Eli stated.

"Two young men lost to senseless violence and a cancer patient that had to be admitted. I think sucked is an understatement," Amara countered. "Sometimes, life is just unfair."

"Dot was a hoot though, wasn't she?" Eli murmured as he let go of her hand and wrapped his arm around her shoulders. "A patient who genuinely makes you laugh is a treasure. And we saved two of the stabbing victims. That's not nothing."

She leaned her head against his, and Eli's soul sang as the soft scent of raspberry shampoo hit his senses. It was weird how the little things about her were still the same.

Amara turned slightly and her eyes met his. Then she closed the distance between their lips. The kiss was light, but it sent a thrill through him as her hands rested on his cheek. It was over far too soon, and Amara eyes were wide and panicked as she leaned away. There had never been anyone else who made him feel the way she did. And once you'd found a person that made you feel whole, it was hard to accept less.

"Sorry, Eli. I—,"

Running a finger along her cheek, Eli interrupted. "Please don't apologize. I've wanted to kiss you since the moment you walked into the ER."

A sigh escaped her lips. "It seems wrong to kiss after such a terrible day." Amara smiled, but he could see the uncertainty that enveloped her.

Eli knew what she meant, but he would never

be sorry for that kiss. For any kiss with Amara. "Life is too short not to reach for every good opportunity. Working in an ER, we know that better than most."

"Life *is* so short." Amara's voice was tight.

There was more to that statement than a bad night on the job, but the parking garage at Boston Gen. wasn't the ideal place to explore it. "I need to get home." Eli squeezed her hand. "Come with me. I have a bad frozen lasagna that I don't mind sharing."

Hesitation hovered in her dark eyes, and Eli told her, "We can swing by your place if you need to feed your cat." He didn't want her to say no.

"I don't have a cat." Amara wiped a final tear from her cheek. "Nothing is waiting for me at home—not even a wilted bag of salad or a bad frozen meal. But I'm tired, and I *should* go home."

Why was she making up a cat when talking to patients?

That was something he was going to find out too.

"Well, I don't know that my well-stocked fridge is my finest asset, but how about we do lunch at my place tomorrow. We can discuss the health fair."

And he could find out exactly what had happened today.

A bit of color flooded her cheeks. What was she thinking? He didn't want her to turn down the offer, and they did need to go over their health care booth. Even if it wasn't his top priority.

"Okay," Amara whispered. "Tomorrow. So, we can discuss the health fair, and I can get some bad lasagna. Or do you want me to bring some decent food."

"I'll handle lunch." Eli winked as he squeezed her hand again. They could talk about the health fair, but Eli was going to find out what had sent her over the edge tonight. If it was something he could fix, he'd do it. Amara belonged at Boston Gen.

With him.

After hesitating a moment, Eli dropped a light kiss against her cheek and then exited from her car.

CHAPTER FIVE

ELI SMILED AS he saw Amara pull into his driveway behind his garage. She'd kissed him last night. It had been amazing and far too short. But the hope the brief kiss had given him was still blazing inside him today.

Having lunch together at his home to talk about the health fair wasn't a date, but his heart pounded as she walked up his driveway. She was really here.

Amara was here.

As he opened the door, Eli nearly tripped as Lizzy rushed at his legs to wave at Amara. It still amazed him how such a tiny child could expend so much force. "Daddy!" She squealed as he lifted her into the air.

His heart sped up as she waved at Lizzy. The toddler stuck her tongue out, and Amara did too. His heart warmed at the simple exchange. Amara had always been good with children; she'd even considered specializing in pediatrics before deciding she loved the ER as much as he did. She'd make a wonderful mother…

Eli shook the thought from his mind. It was true. But it was also way too soon.

"She's very swift for someone with such tiny legs." His mom rounded the corner. She grinned as she saw Amara. His mother had always loved her, but Martha had understood better than anyone else why she'd walked away. She'd told him this morning to be very careful. His mother loved Marshall, but she'd finally divorced him.

Tired of living alone in her marriage.

Those words had sent a chill through Eli when Martha had told him and Sam of her decision five years ago. Amara had worried that she'd be lonely if she stayed with him too, so she'd left. But he wouldn't make the same mistake his father had. He'd find a way to balance his professional goals and family responsibilities, so nothing suffered.

"It's nice to see you again," Martha said. "Thank you for coming to my art show. That was incredibly sweet."

"I enjoyed it. You're very talented." Amara stated as his mom pulled her into an unexpected hug.

Martha turned to Lizzy. "Come to Oma." She

laughed as Lizzy launched into her arms. "We're going to the park now."

Eli dropped a light kiss on the top of Lizzy's head before hugging his mom. Then he turned to Amara. "Hope you're hungry. I ordered some roasted tomato pasta." Eli nodded toward the kitchen.

"That sounds much better than a frozen lasagna," Amara teased.

"Or wilted salad." Eli winked as he pulled a few plates from a cupboard.

"Bagged salad is easy. My kitchen is tiny and cooking for one…" Amara cleared her throat as she stared out the small window, "I always end up with more leftovers than I can eat."

Before he could comment, Amara rushed on. "Besides, bagged salad is better than vending machine snacks." Her nose scrunched up.

He hated that she didn't cook much anymore. Amara had loved cooking. More than one person had stopped by to ask for a recipe as delicious scents floated from their windows. "You're free to use this kitchen anytime." The words slipped from Eli's lips, and he was rewarded with a brilliant smile.

"You shouldn't offer that up so lightly! I'll have

this place smelling like lemon rice in no time."
She laughed, her eyes holding his.

"I love lemon rice." Eli couldn't stop the grin
from spreading across his face too. Amara had
always been able to make him happy. Whether
he was buried in med school homework, stressed
about his family, or dealing with a bad night at
the ER, Amara simply made things better.

Amara stood against the kitchen counter as Eli
piled tomatoes and pasta onto large blue plates.
He was dressed casually, in jeans that hugged his
backside perfectly and a green T-shirt. Stubble
covered his jaw, and she sighed. Eli looked delicious.

She hadn't meant to kiss him last night, but she
was surprised that she didn't regret it. She'd almost agreed to follow him home last night too,
but she'd managed to catch herself. Lunch to talk
about the health fair had felt safer…but it wasn't.

Not really.

Her stomach twisted as he stared at her. Why
was she trying to kid herself? She wanted to be
near him.

Needed to be near him.

She was still worried about ending up like her

mother, loving a man who was too busy to see her—to love her back. But Eli was busier now than he had been a decade ago, and he'd made time for her. They'd shared tacos, looked at community art, he'd delivered tea to her, and last night when he'd held her as she cried, another bit of the wall she'd built around her heart crumbled.

They were older now, wiser, more sure of themselves. Maybe a second chance could work between them...*maybe*. Then a little voice prodded at her.

He still didn't know about her double mastectomy, did he?

"Do you want me to make a pot of tea? I also have soda, and I am pretty sure Lizzy wouldn't mind you sneaking some of her milk," Eli said as he set a plate before her and wandered back to the stove.

"Water works." Amara's eyes gleamed. "I wouldn't want to steal milk from such a cutie." She pulled back a stool and sat. "Lizzy really is adorable."

"She is," Eli agreed as he set his plate on the counter and sat beside her. "So, I have an important question."

What did he want to know? Amara's stomach

flipped. Once Eli had known everything about her. Did she want him to know everything again? Even the bits she found difficult to talk about?

Yes, maybe, she thought indecisively.

"Ask away."

"Why are you making up a cat?"

She tilted her head as Eli's masculine scent teased her nostrils. He smelled just like she remembered—*like home.* Focusing hard, she stared into his dark chocolate eyes. "I didn't make Pepper up. He was an incredible cat who liked to tip glasses off the counter far too often. I got very tired of cleaning broken pottery, so all my cups are still plastic. But I lost him not long ago."

Amara set her fork down, smiling as she remembered Pepper's antics. "I still tell funny stories about him at work. It helps patients relax—especially children."

Eli gripped her hand. The touch was comforting, but as his thumb rubbed the delicate skin on her wrist, she wanted to pull him close. What would he do if she kissed him again? Really kissed him this time?

Her skin lit up as he held her hand. Such a simple touch, but it made her crave so much more. She'd lain awake last night, replaying those moments. Questioning herself for kissing him. Kicking herself for not kissing him again, more deeply.

Eli's dark eyes were lit with an emotion she wanted to believe was desire. "I was convinced your cat had really destroyed your breakfast by tipping milk into your eggs." Eli chuckled.

Amara laughed too. "That was Pepper's favorite trick. Though I admit that when I'm trying to calm an adult, I change the milk to coffee."

"You actually started drinking coffee? Why have I been bringing you tea?" Eli protested and leaned and close.

If she moved a few inches, she could kiss him again. Was that what he was hoping she'd do? Amara frowned as she pushed back at the desire building in her belly. "Nope. Sorry to disappoint you."

"You could never disappoint me."

His words were soft, but they struck her hard. What would he think of her scars? Would they disappoint him? Worry stabbed at her brain again, and she pulled away.

She cleared her throat, then shrugged. "Coffee works better with adults."

"Because that's what adults drink." Eli's smile

wasn't as wide as before, but he didn't release her hand.

And she didn't pull it back.

"How is your mom? There is a specialty grocery down the street, and I stop in to grab naan bread a few times a month. I tried to make her chicken curry once, do you remember? It was a disaster."

Amara swallowed. It was a reasonable question; Eli had no way of knowing how much it would hurt her to answer him. She squeezed his hand, drawing strength from the heat of his body. "Mom passed a little over three years ago." Amara bit her lip as tears coated her eyes. Why was this still so hard for her to talk about?

Eli held her gaze as he reached for her other hand. "What happened?"

"Breast cancer. By the time Mom finally went to the doctor, she was already stage four," Amara said.

"That's why you reacted so strongly to Seth's cancer yesterday."

"Yes."

And no.

She should tell him that she'd learned of her own cancer risk and alleviated as much of it as she could. But she feared he'd look at her like Joe had. Or rather, stop looking at her at all.

The more time she spent with Eli, the more she realized how different she was with him. Relaxed, happy, *ready to love*... But she refused to examine that thought too closely.

"I took care of her. Was there for every step of her treatment and the final decisions she had to make. My father was too busy. Some business deal in California. He barely made it back in time for the funeral and waited less than three months to remarry." She couldn't hide the anger as the words flew from her lips. Amara was surprised by how much she wanted to talk to Eli about this. Joe hadn't wanted to hear it, and she hadn't wanted to share it. But with Eli...

"After she passed, I felt so alone. Then the man I was seeing ended our relationship. Actually, Joe chose someone new before telling me we were over." Amara shook her head. She hadn't meant to lay any of this at Eli's feet. She never usually unloaded on others. Except she always had with Eli.

"I am so sorry, Amara. But you're not alone now," Eli whispered as he held her gaze.

"At least for today," Amara said, trying to find

a way to lighten the mood as she skewered a tomato. "Though I could definitely be bribed to return for this."

"Then I will ask Mom for the recipe and practice cooking it whenever I have a chance." His cell buzzed, and Eli silenced it. But it immediately started buzzing again. "Guess Marshall really needs something." Eli squeezed her hand. "I won't be long."

Amara squashed the tinge of worry in her belly. It was just a phone call from his father. Eli was raising Lizzy, and it was obvious from the little girl's smiles that Eli had changed. He spent as much time with her as possible. He made sure to be at his mother's art shows, and he hadn't given in to his father's demands to become a surgeon.

Eli was back in less than five minutes. "Sorry, Amara. Marshall will call or text twenty times a day for a week, then I won't hear from him for a month. Now he's asked me to up my role at the research group. Even though I'm not a surgeon."

"You're an amazing doctor." Amara hated the uncertainty she saw crossing Eli's face.

"Thanks." Eli's lips brushed her cheek as he grabbed the dishes and took them to the sink.

Without thinking, Amara moved to stand beside him and wrapped her arms around him. "I bet you'll do wonderful things for the company. Have you put your notice in at Boston Gen.?" She didn't want him to go, but Eli could do good work at his father's research group.

"Of course not. Marshall still practices several days a week. I can do both. I already have been doing both and raising Lizzy." Eli's brows were knit as he filled the sink with water and dish detergent.

His words sent a flash of concern down Amara's spine. Grabbing a dish towel, she dried the dishes Eli washed. Tapping his hip with hers, Amara said, "You can't do it all, Eli. And that's okay. You're already remarkable, you know."

"Remarkable?" Eli raised an eyebrow. "If you keep those compliments coming, I may never stop smiling."

Amara shook her head. She was glad the statement made him happy, but if he was doing so much, something would break.

And then he'd blame himself.

"I'm serious."

"I know. But it's only part-time, Amara. Mostly I'm reading research grants on my couch. I'm not sleeping at the office, I promise. But I don't want to talk about Marshall anymore."

Amara let out a sigh and laid the towel on the counter. "What would you like to discuss?" She'd come to talk about the health fair, after all.

"Do you ever wonder what would have happened if I hadn't let you walk away?"

"What?" *Yes.* That's what she should have said, but that word was caught in her throat.

"Do you ever think about us? Wonder what-if?" Eli's words were soft as his eyes raked across her face.

"All the time." The truth finally slipped out, and she stepped into his arms. Whatever happened, this was where she wanted to be right now.

The smell of his cologne cascaded over her. His head lowered. His kiss was soft, not demanding, but a part of her heart knit together as he held her. This was where she'd belonged so long ago.

Wanted to belong again.

Eli broke the kiss and pushed a bit of hair away from her cheek. "I should have promised you what you needed then. I wanted to, but I was too caught up in the lure of being like Marshall.

Better. I still want Boston General to be in the national rankings, but I don't need it like I did. Give me a second chance, Amara. Give us a second chance. Please."

What was she supposed to say? So many thoughts were running through her mind. "What if you never make the list, or if Boston Gen. doesn't?" She loved their hospital, but its administration wasn't interested in courting editors to achieve rankings.

"I want to tell you that it won't matter, but I suspect it will always sting a bit. But I'm not going to give up time with Lizzy, and hopefully, you, to chase that dream. Life is too short, and these last few weeks, I realize how much my life was missing something. It was missing you."

Eli ran a hand through his hair. "Lizzy and I are going to the zoo day after tomorrow. Want to come with us?" He reached for her hand. "It'll be fun and probably a little crazy with a toddler in tow." Eli shrugged. "It could be a date or just…"

Amara dropped a light kiss on his lips. "It's a date. What time?" Maybe she was being reckless with her heart, but she didn't want to tell him no. There'd also been a hole in her life since she'd walked away from Eli. It disappeared when she was with him, and Amara didn't want it to re-open.

A brilliant smile spread across Eli's face. "How about I pick you up at nine? That way, we're there when the zoo opens and can see a good portion before Lizzy needs her afternoon nap."

"Sounds good."

"I just need your number." He laughed, "That sounds so weird." He ran his hand through his hair again.

Amara lifted her cell and opened her contacts. "Have you changed yours since college?" She'd never been able to delete his number.

Despite their parting, the thought of severing that final connection to Eli had always made her cry. He was too important to just wipe away forever. She'd looked at it multiple times, almost dialed it a few times too. Which was why DO NOT CALL was written in the Business Name section under his name.

The expression in his eyes sent a thrill down her spine. "Nope." He grabbed his own phone and sent a text that immediately pinged on her phone's screen.

She stared at the silly emoji. "Guess we're

good then." Amara's heart leaped as she leaned toward him; Eli hadn't deleted her number either.

"We're home," Martha called.

Amara jumped back.

His mom's eyes flicked between Eli and Amara, and she winced. "Sorry. Lizzy was falling asleep in the swing. I didn't…"

"It's fine," Amara squeaked. "I needed to get going anyway. We can discuss the health fair after the zoo. Or at the hospital." She hesitated only a moment before dropping a light kiss on his cheek. "Thanks for lunch, Eli."

CHAPTER SIX

ELI PULLED AT the collar of his shirt for the sixth time. He'd changed once already and was feeling more ridiculous by the minute. There was no reason to feel nervous; it was just a trip to the zoo, wasn't it?

He shook his head. Dating jitters had never plagued him before. Except, this wasn't just a date with Amara.

Today could be the start of a new chapter for them. And Eli was going to make sure Amara had a great time.

His phone buzzed with a text from Marshall, and Eli sent a quick response. He waited a minute and then added a note that he'd be at the zoo with Amara and Lizzy and unavailable. He wasn't sure Marshall understood what that meant, but his father's texts and calls had been never-ending the last two days. However, today Eli was just going to enjoy the perfect weather outside with Amara and Lizzy.

Amara's text pinged into his phone.

Want me to pack any snacks?

Nope. I got this!

He could balance everything. She'd see.

He smiled as she sent back a thumbs-up icon. The connection he felt with Amara hadn't been present with anyone else. Eli had always assumed his memory was mistaken and had reinforced an ideal that hadn't existed.

But it wasn't.

"Momma!" Lizzy screamed as Eli grabbed her diaper bag and picked her up.

His heart broke as Lizzy looked at the door. Eli kissed her cheek and redirected her attention. "We're going to see monkeys." Eli tapped her nose to make her laugh. "We just have to stop and get Amara first."

Lizzy's small face puckered as she stared at him. Eli knew she didn't completely understand what he meant, but he sighed in relief when she snuggled against his chest. He'd never realized how much parenting was flying by the seat of your pants, doubting easy choices and gathering as many snuggles as possible. It was exhilarating, exhausting and perfection.

Ruffling Lizzy's curly dark hair, Eli tried to calm his nerves. The weather was perfect, and Amara was coming. Today was going to be fun.

Eli's skin tingled as his eyes landed on Amara. She was dressed in a lightweight gray tank top and blue shorts, and her dark hair was pulled into a side braid. She waved and he grinned.

Amara hustled to the car, giving him a quick kiss before turning to smile at Lizzy. "Hi, cutie!"

Her cinnamon and tea scent flooded his senses. "We would have come up to get you," Eli said. "You didn't have to wait on the sidewalk for us. Or are you hiding something in your apartment?"

Amara shook her head. "Not hiding anything. I'm just excited to go to the zoo."

He saw her cheeks heat as she returned Lizzy's wave. She was obviously just as excited as he was for today. "I'm really looking forward to it too." He laid his hand on her knee before brushing his lips against hers, relishing the moment.

"Monkeys!" Lizzy screamed from the backseat.

Amara's fingers rubbed her lips as she stared

at him. "I think someone wants to go see the monkeys."

Lizzy clapped her hands and shouted, "Monkeys," again.

Perhaps a zoo date with a toddler hadn't been such a great idea. But Eli wanted Amara to get to know Lizzy. Wanted Amara to see that *he* understood the importance of family now.

"Monkeys, here we come." Eli exclaimed as they headed out.

They were on a date...

And a light kiss, barely more than a peck, was enough to make her blood sing. She'd thought of kissing Eli nearly every free minute of the last two days. That should thrill her.

But she was still hiding an important part of herself. Amara wasn't ashamed of her new body. It was healthy, and her reconstructive surgeon had done an excellent job, but she still looked different. It had bothered Joe so much. He'd looked at her like she was broken when she'd healed, then found comfort with another woman. If Eli ever looked at her that way...

Amara knew she should tell him—wanted to tell him. But the words had never found their way into any of their conversations. The everyday banter they'd shared had been easier. *Safer.*

This might not be a traditional date, but here with Eli was right where Amara wanted to be. She couldn't seem to stop smiling. Lifting Lizzy, she held her up to see the monkeys, careful to keep her far enough away from the glass that she couldn't bang on it.

"Monkeys," Lizzy squealed and laughed as Eli snapped a few pictures.

"You're going to fill up your phone with pictures of her." Amara grinned as Eli snapped a few more. The happiness in his eyes was contagious.

"Not just of her." Eli showed her the screen. He'd caught an image of Amara laughing with Lizzy and a monkey watching them in the background. "Hard to tell who's having more fun. Lizzy, you or the monkey," Eli teased.

Then his phone buzzed, and Amara saw him immediately shift from Eli back to Dr. Collins. She'd watched her father do that too, whenever his work called. But they weren't on call this weekend, and her phone was still blessedly silent. "Everything okay?"

"Marshall's texting. He wants me to go over some documents later."

"Really?" She tried to keep her voice light. Amara had known when she'd agreed to this date that Eli was already splitting his time between so many projects. It would be disingenuous to complain now. "Hopefully, it's nothing urgent."

"It's always urgent. At least, according to Marshall." Eli winked and then made a show of turning his phone off. "But I'm off the clock today."

Amara's heart raced as Eli placed the phone in his back pocket. Her father had never turned his off. He'd barely ever looked away from it. Her mother used to say that if she needed to speak to her husband, she had to video call him—even if they were in the same house.

Her mom had laughed, but Amara had seen the hurt behind it. Eli putting away his connection to the outside world for a few hours meant more than he realized.

Amara was glad Marshall, or anyone else, couldn't interrupt them, but Eli's phone was also a camera and she didn't want him to miss out any memories. "What about taking more pictures of this cutie?"

Eli looked at his niece. "Today, we'll just have

to rely on our memory—like in olden times." He laughed. "Perhaps it's time to invest in an actual digital camera, though. Then I can fill up my phone's memory card *and* the camera's memory with pictures."

Amara grinned as he made faces with Lizzy. Even with his overloaded schedule, Amara doubted Eli would forget Lizzy's birthday or miss every dance recital like her father had. Eli was a committed dad, but would he be as committed to her?

Her heart wanted to believe it, needed to believe it, but her brain still urged her to be cautious. This was, after all, only one perfect day in a few weeks of good times. What would happen in a few months or even years? Particularly if neither he nor Boston General received the recognition he wanted?

Lizzy gripped their hands as they walked toward the prairie dog exhibit, and Amara looked at the little girl. "Want us to swing you?" Amara laughed as Lizzy looked at her with surprise.

"I used to love it when my grandmother and mom would swing me when I was little, in grocery store parking lots and even at the zoo. If my fuzzy memory remembers right," Amara explained. She winked at Eli before looking at Lizzy. "Just hold on tight."

As Lizzy's peals of laughter rang out, his gaze bored through Amara. Her skin tingled, and her heart pounded so fast, she thought it was trying to fly from her chest. This was the definition of happiness. This was the life she'd always wanted, the life she'd craved.

With Eli.

"Again!" Lizzy shouted.

"That does have a tendency to happen," Amara said as Eli's eyes sparkled. He was an incredible dad and an amazing doctor.

He was just perfect.

Lizzy clapped as they walked into the petting zoo, then yawned. The day had been lovely, but the little one was quickly losing her ability to stay awake. Amara suspected the toddler would be asleep before they got to the parking lot.

"I'm going to buy some food," Eli said. "Then, we can feed the goats."

"Why don't we see how she does with the goats first?" Amara suggested. "We can always bring her back another day…" Amara made the offer without thinking; still, it felt right. She'd come to the zoo with Lizzy and Eli anytime he asked.

But Eli had already started toward the small hut where a bored teenager was handing out cups of goat pellets. Amara grinned. Eli was having just as much fun, if not more, than his niece.

He was a natural at parenting, even if he over-thought birthday cakes. Her heart pounded as she stared at him. If they worked out as a couple this time, would he want more children?

That thought sent a blast of panic through her. Eli had been back in Amara's life for a little over a month, and she was already thinking about family. Wondering what if… Because that was what Amara had always dreamed of.

A family.

But happy families took work and time. Still, Eli had promised he would put them first. *No*, she remembered. He'd promised he could balance his responsibilities perfectly—his patients, his work for the Collins Research Group *and* his family. Could he keep that promise? If he didn't, was she strong enough to demand it, or walk away?

Biting her lip, Amara held Lizzy as she studied the goats.

Stop worrying, she ordered herself.

Before she'd passed, her mother had warned Amara that constant worrying wouldn't stop the future from happening and only resulted in regrets. Amara wanted to live life without fear, but what if she made the wrong choice and got hurt…again?

Eli's arm slid around Amara's waist, and some of her worry fell away. Eli was here now; that's what she should focus on. As he held up the cup of pellets, his warm gaze pushed the last of her doubts to the back of her mind.

They entered the goat pen, and Amara barely managed to control her *I told you so* when Lizzy refused to get down. The little girl wanted to see the goats but had no desire to pet one. Or use the goat food that Eli had purchased.

"It will be fun." He held up the cup and tried to coax Lizzy to take it.

"No!" Lizzy shouted before she buried her head in Amara's shoulder.

"Want to watch Daddy feed the goats?" Amara suggested and was rewarded with a nod.

Lizzy's giggles were contagious as Eli marched over to the biggest goat. The goat grabbed for the cup, and Eli jumped as the animal quickly gobbled everything in sight.

"Well, that went fast. I'm going to find a trash can," Eli said as Lizzy yawned—again. "Then we should probably head home."

Amara leaned against the petting zoo fence as she held Lizzy. With Eli gone, the goats quickly lost the last of their appeal to the toddler. After a few minutes, Amara turned to look for Eli. The sun was bright, but she could see a trash can less than thirty feet from her.

Where was he?

"Charles Xavier!" The mother's screech tore through the petting zoo. "Get back here!"

Before Amara could react, a young boy bowled into them as he rushed toward the goats. She gripped Lizzy to her chest but couldn't keep her balance. Pain ripped down Amara's left arm and stars danced in her eyes as Lizzy screamed. Despite the pain, she managed to control her fall enough to blunt any injury to the little girl.

"Amara! I'm so sorry." Eli was suddenly next to her, reaching for Lizzy.

Tears stung her eyes, and her derriere was more than a mite sore from the tumble. And her arm burned. As Amara touched her shoulder, she was surprised when her fingers came away covered in blood.

The cut ran from the top of her shoulder to an inch above her elbow. Amara stared up at the fence and glared at a nail she hadn't noticed. She had landed just right to catch the stupid thing. This was not the way she'd wanted the day to end.

Breathing through the pain, she let Eli examine her arm while she kissed the top of Lizzy's head, trying to comfort her as well as she could with one hand.

"I think you need a few stitches." Eli pushed his hand through his hair. "I'm so sorry," he repeated.

"Did you push us?" she asked.

Eli's mouth fell open, but he still looked worried. "What?"

Why did this bother him so much? It was an unfortunate accident that no one could have foreseen. "You've apologized twice for a kid getting excited and accidentally pushing us over. Or are you apologizing for my unluckiness to catch a barely exposed nail just right? This is as far from being your fault as possible."

His eyes shifted a bit as he brushed a loose

piece of hair from her face. "You'll need stitches and a tetanus booster."

"Eli." Amara pressed her closed fist to his shoulder, trying to offer some form of comfort without getting blood on him. "I'm going to be fine. I promise."

Eli pulled a T-shirt from Lizzy's diaper bag and pressed it against the wound. "Guess it's a good thing I always pack a change of clothes in case she gets messy."

"Yes." Amara winced as she held the shirt against her shoulder. "Hopefully, this isn't a favorite outfit."

"Nope," Eli stated as he helped Amara to her feet and picked up Lizzy. "We need to get you to Boston Gen."

Amara flinched as another bout of pain shot down her arm. "Not an ideal way to end our date."

"The next one is going to end better," Eli promised.

Next one.

Amara sighed as he wrapped an arm around her. "You're getting blood on your shirt."

"I don't care." Eli kissed her forehead as Lizzy reached for Amara.

The toddler's small demand made her want to beam with joy. Despite their tumble, Lizzy was fine and still wanted Amara to hold her. She'd enjoyed their zoo date, even if it was ending with a few stitches.

"Amara hurt her shoulder, sweetheart. We have to go get her looked at." Eli frowned as they walked from the petting zoo. "I really am so sorry, Amara."

Since she was holding Lizzy's shirt against her arm, Amara couldn't hold his hand, but she leaned her head against his shoulder. "Don't worry."

Eli couldn't believe he was sitting in Boston Gen.'s waiting room with Amara. Technically, he knew he wasn't responsible for the accident. But if he'd just dumped the cup in the trash and come right back, they'd have been halfway to the car by the time the other child had reached the petting zoo.

Instead, he'd stepped away and checked his phone.

After he'd made such a big deal about turning it off.

And then he'd sent a handful of texts back to Marshall.

He probably shouldn't care what his father thought. Eli knew that, but after years of almost no communication, he wanted to help Marshall now that he'd asked for Eli's assistance. To prove to him that he was a great physician. If he never made the rankings like Marshall had, knowing his father respected him would be enough.

When he'd heard Lizzy scream, Eli had raced back and felt his stomach drop at the blood traveling down Amara's arm. "If they'd just let me put a few stitches in your arm, we'd have been out of here hours ago," he grumbled. At least his mother had picked up Lizzy.

He sighed as Amara leaned her head against him. If they were pretty much anywhere else but here, this would feel perfect.

"You're not on the clock. I'm sure Griffin or one of the other doctors will be free soon." Amara pecked his cheek. "Patience is a virtue."

Not one he'd ever excelled at.

"How is it feeling?" Eli asked.

"Like a nail cut into my skin." Amara sighed. "Sorry, Eli. I know you're upset, but at least we have a fun story to tell."

"A fun story?" He raised his hands and gestured to the gray walls of the waiting area. "Not sure this really counts."

"Sure, we can tell people how I saved Lizzy from a rampaging goat, while you were off scouting a long-lost trash can."

Her laughter was contagious, and Eli joined in despite the guilt racing through him. "I don't think that's how it happened."

Except for the part where he'd been too far away to help.

"When you told me that Lizzy hated going to sleep, I thought you were kidding. She really is passionately against bedtime," Amara said. They'd picked Lizzy up from his mom's apartment on their way home from Boston Gen.

Despite the seven stitches in her arm, Amara wasn't sure she'd change anything about today. Spending the entire day with Eli had quieted most of her worries. She was glad they'd had the health fair to discuss because Amara hadn't wanted their time together to end. She wasn't sure she'd ever get enough of spending time with Lizzy and Eli.

"Lizzy lures you in with her cuteness, never

showing the monster beneath it—until bedtime," Eli teased and dropped a light kiss on her lips as he passed her a grilled cheese sandwich.

Her heart felt like it might explode. The kiss wasn't enough. Amara wanted more, so much more. But their stomachs growled, almost in unison, and she laughed. There would be plenty of time for kisses later—*there would.*

"I think all toddlers are tiny adorable monsters." Amara sat next to Eli on the couch, enjoying the warmth coming off him.

He took a few bites of his sandwich before wrapping an arm around her shoulders—careful to avoid the line of stitches. "No, but she does have a stubborn streak. Reminds me of my brother." Eli chuckled.

"So, you and Sam had the same stubborn streak?" Amara asked as Eli put his hand over his heart, pretending she'd wounded him.

Eli nodded. "I prefer to think of the quality as 'determined' when it's me."

"Determined?" Amara whispered, enjoying the slow smile spreading across his face. If she kissed the delicate skin along his collarbone, would Eli still groan and pull her close? Amara felt her cheeks heat as she stared at his lips. They were so near.

"Should we discuss the health fair?" Eli asked huskily. "Or, is there something else you might like do?" His finger slid along her jaw.

As his gaze swept her body, panic raced across her skin. She still hadn't mentioned the scars across her chest. Or the reasons she'd elected to have a preventative double mastectomy. She needed to...and now was the perfect time. Or at least as good as any. But as the memory of Joe's reaction danced behind her eyelids, the words refused to materialize.

"Health fair," she squeaked, hating the touch of anxiety racing through her.

"Oh...right," Eli said before withdrawing his arm and grabbing her empty plate. "Just let me get my notes."

Amara took several deep breaths, trying to calm the rush of emotions tumbling through her.

I had a surgery that drastically changed the odds that I'll get breast cancer despite my genetic markers. But it means I look different from the last time we were together.

Those words should be so easy to state. Eli

was a physician, he'd understand. But Joe was a doctor, as well…

Eli returned with a giant binder and laid it out on the coffee table. Amara hated that she was grateful to have a reason to put off the conversation a bit longer.

"This is what I've done for the last few years. Each year the booth is different, so we need to pick a theme and then look for a giveaway and…"

The binder had more tabs in it than most patient folders. Amara stared at it. When he'd mentioned that he'd won each year, she'd hadn't realized Eli was planning a major event. "Woah…wait, I thought we'd partner with a local health agency like the American Cancer Society or the Red Cross."

"The health fair draws attention to Boston General. The better the booths, the more attention, and the better chance someone nominates us for awards," Eli stated as he flipped through the binder, not looking at her.

Grabbing the binder, Amara laid it in her lap. "That is a lot of pressure to put on a health fair."

On himself.

"And unrealistic to boot!" Eli hid his insecurities better than he had years ago, but they were clearly still there—bubbling just under the surface.

"No, it's not." Eli's voice was tense. "Community involvement might be one of the criteria for getting on the list." Eli pushed his hand through his hair as his eyes held hers.

Amara wished there was a way to make him see himself, truly see himself. He was a great doctor, no matter what a stupid list said. Stroking his cheek, Amara took a deep breath. "You don't know the criteria for the thing that you're chasing after? That's a bit crazy, Eli."

"I've tried to figure out the criteria for years, but it's been a bit elusive." Eli gripped her hands and added, "I even asked Marshall, since he's been on the list a dozen times. But he just said someone nominated him." Eli smiled.

It was so close to a grimace, Amara's heart shook. Eli was chasing a goal with no known path to success. That could drive anyone to madness.

Shifting the conversation, she asked, "What did you do with all the extra vacation days you won?"

"What?" His eyes roamed from her to the closed binder. "Why?"

His defensiveness worried her. He was requesting shifts off to see his mother's art shows. Surely Eli was taking his vacation days? He reached for the binder in her lap, but she held it tightly.

Eli raised an eyebrow as he reached around her. "Come on, Amara. Let me have my notes."

She stood and moved to the other side of the room. "No. Not until you tell me what you used your extra vacation days for last year. Did you go to Rome or Scotland? What about California or Hawaii?"

Eli's lips turned down, and she wanted to shake him. "Did you go skiing? Or hiking?" She knew the answer, but she hoped she was wrong. "The beach? A resort? Eli?"

When he still refused to say anything, Amara dropped the binder on the floor, ignoring the thump it made. "What did you do with the days you earned by putting so much effort into your booth for a grand prize you might never get?"

He looked away. "Nothing. At the end of last year, I had ten unused vacation days that I forfeited. Are you happy now?"

The dismal statement broke her heart. Why would he ask her that? "Of course not."

Amara returned to the couch and wrapped her

arms around him. Her breath hitched as his fingers ran along the back of her spine. She was not going to let his soft touch distract her.

"We used to talk about traveling all the time. Remember those silly guidebooks?" Amara grinned as a bit of the tension eased from Eli's features. "Now you're earning extra vacation days and not using them. You're following your father's path, but don't have the map."

Amara put her finger over his lips before he could interrupt. "You are one of the top doctors at Boston Gen. You could work anywhere. You're a wonderful, attentive father, an impressive doctor and gorgeous. You do not need to be on some artificial list to prove your worth. You can chart your own course now." Amara gripped his knee. "You *are* enough, Eli." It was the truth.

If only she could make him see it.

"Gorgeous?" Eli asked and raised an eyebrow.

"All the compliments I give you, and that's the one you focus on." Amara playfully rolled her eyes. Her chest tightened as Eli leaned toward her. He was so close, and she'd missed him so much. Her heart pounded as she stared at his full lips.

Eli pushed a lock of hair behind her ear, his

fingers lingering just a bit along her jaw. "If we win, I promise to take a vacation this year."

"If we win, I'll make sure you do," Amara whispered. Her stomach rolled with desire, nervousness and hope. "A real one. With no cell phones, research papers. No work!"

"I missed you so much," Eli stated simply, and her world came undone.

She kissed him then. He still tasted of honey, sunlight, comfort and longing.

Her Eli...

They'd once felt like two halves of a whole. Could they again?

Her fingers ran along his shoulders as he pulled her closer, as if Eli couldn't accept any space between them either. This was the kiss Amara had wanted for days, weeks...years. The one that spoke of all their mutual longing. The kiss that demonstrated how much passion they still felt for one another. It was everything.

Eli's fingers dipped along the side of her breasts, and she froze. If they didn't stop now, where would the night lead? The thought tore through her as she pulled away. "I should leave."

"Amara." Eli took her hands. "Stay...please."

She wanted to, desperately. But staying meant

so much more than planning for the health fair. Kisses, promises…maybe the hope of forever clung to Eli. She wanted all of it, but the fear that he'd look at her differently once he found out about her surgery clung to her too. Fear that this happiness could evaporate in an instant ripped through her. She just needed a bit more time.

Amara removed her hands from his, stood and reached for her purse. "I'm going to brainstorm some themes for our booth."

"Can we discuss the health fair over dinner tomorrow?"

Amara shook her head. "We're on shift tomorrow evening."

"I know. But if there's a break, we are having dinner. I'm not sure what happened just now…"

"Eli." Amara frowned.

"It's okay." He stood and pressed his lips to each of her cheeks before lightly kissing her lips. "Whenever you're ready, you'll tell me."

Her eyes clouded with tears. "I'll see you tomorrow." It was a promise, and behind it lay so many more. Amara grabbed her keys and barely kept her feet moving forward.

CHAPTER SEVEN

AMARA WISHED SHE hadn't panicked last night as she walked through the doors of Boston Gen. the next morning. That she'd found the right words to tell him about her surgery. Eli wasn't like the other men she'd dated since her double mastectomy. But she couldn't stop the fear.

Amara had stood before a mirror last night and stared at the scars across her chest. They'd faded in the three years since her surgery. The skin was still tucked, and the nipples she'd had tattooed on would never look exactly like her previous ones had. The memory of Joe's averted gaze threatened to overwhelm her.

It didn't matter now, she tried to tell herself.

She automatically performed a quick search for Eli, but he wasn't in the hall. She'd figured out what they should do for the health fair, laid out some plans, grabbed him a coffee and now she just had to find him.

"Are you doing okay with Eli and the health

fair?" Susan asked as she followed Amara into the lounge.

Amara was surprised by the look of concern on Susan's face. "Still planning, but I want to focus on healthy eating and do a cooking demonstration." She just needed to get Eli on board. This idea was different from any he'd ever done, but she was almost certain he'd like it.

Almost...

"Well, I'd do the cooking demonstration. Eli likes to joke that he really shouldn't be allowed near a stove. Though he does make a very passable grilled cheese." Amara chuckled as she leaned against the locker, memories of last night making her smile.

If only she hadn't run.

"He'll probably try to convince you to hire a celebrity chef." Susan's brows furrowed as she stared at Amara.

A celebrity chef for the health fair? That seemed over the top, even for Eli. "Why would he do that?" Amara asked as she placed her stethoscope around her neck.

"To draw attention to Boston Gen." Susan shrugged.

"I know he wants people to see this hospital

for the fine institution it is, but a celebrity chef is ridiculous for a community health fair." Amara knew Eli wanted outside recognition. But she still hoped that he didn't *need* it like he once had. After all, he seemed happy with his life now.

"I'm not so sure. He's done a lot for this place in the last six years, but we will never be Massachusetts Research." Susan sighed. "That place chases awards like it's their job."

Amara nodded. "That's true." She'd worked there for nearly a decade. But she knew why Eli cared about those accolades so much. It made her heart ache that he clearly still wrestled with stepping outside of his father's shadow. And Marshall didn't make his son's struggle any easier. He asked Eli for help, called and texted at all hours, but never offered a thank-you or told Eli he'd done well. As soon as one task was completed, Marshall focused on the next, barely seeing the people around him. Eli was chasing an approval Amara feared was never going to come.

"I paired you with him because I figured he would just take over." Susan shrugged. "I assumed Eli would handle everything, and you'd get a few extra vacation days. I know the hospital doesn't offer great starting packages, even for nurses with your résumé. Instead, it appears you've helped him take a desperately needed chill pill. I'm impressed."

Amara swallowed. "I have?"

Susan winked. "This time last year, half the nursing staff wanted to murder him. He and Dr. Stanfred kept goading each other. The fact that Eli never uses the vacation days he wins drives Griffin insane."

Leaning against the locker bank, Susan studied Amara. "You're a calming influence on him." Adjusting her purse, she patted Amara's arm. "Now, if you'll excuse me, my very handsome dinner date is waiting for me."

Eli stepped into the lounge and waved at Susan as she walked out. His dark hair was a bit mussed, but he looked amazing. His eyes met Amara's, and light danced across them.

She'd never get tired of that reaction. *Never.* Amara handed him his coffee. "I know what we should do for the health fair." She knew it was a good idea, but Susan's worries had crawled into her head.

"I think we should do a cooking demonstration." She grabbed her notes and passed them to

Eli. She kept talking as he looked over the stack of recipes she'd compiled last night. "I pulled my mom's old recipes. They're healthy, most are vegetarian, so that cuts out the cost of meat, and the rest of the ingredients are inexpensive staples. We can hand out samples and a pamphlet with the cooking instructions."

She held her breath. Amara knew this wasn't a fancy booth like he'd planned before. "I can handle most of it—you'll just show up as my helper." Eli kept his focus on the recipes. "I know this is different—"

"It's perfect," Eli interrupted.

His broad smile sent waves of hope and happiness floating through her. He was letting her take over the booth, and she could cook her mother's recipes. Her mom would have loved that—basked in the glory of it even. "I do need one thing, though."

"What? If it's in my power, the answer is yes."

"I haven't cooked these dishes in a while, and I need to adjust the recipes so I can make larger batches…"

"You need my kitchen." Eli's eyes darkened with desire as they looked at her lips.

"Yes," she whispered. If she was over at his

place, they'd kiss again. She wanted to, so badly, but anxiety knotted her stomach once again. "I'd need to be there several times a week to get all the recipes perfected. I don't want to impose."

Eli gripped her hand. "That sounds very much like the opposite of imposition to me. I want you to visit."

The sounds of sirens echoed in the hall, and Eli put his coffee on top of a locker. "Duty calls."

They moved together toward the bay, and Amara barely managed to contain her surprise as Marshall stepped out of the back of the ambulance. She heard Eli's intake of breath, but he didn't hesitate like she did as the paramedics lowered the patient from the ambulance.

"What happened?" Eli asked the paramedic.

"Gillian found Tabitha passed out on the floor, her face slack," Marshall answered.

Stroke... The word raced through Amara's head, and she saw Eli nod.

"The mobile CT scanner is in trauma 2," Eli called. "That's where we're headed, people."

"You need to remain here, Dr. Collins." Eli's voice was tight as he followed Amara.

"Like hell, I will!" Marshall exclaimed.

"Tabitha's been with The Collins Research Group for almost two decades. She'd want me—"

"She's coding, Eli!" Amara pulled out the shock paddles and started to pass them to Eli, but Marshall was in the way.

Eli reached around his father and grabbed the paddles from her. "You don't have visiting physician rights at Boston Gen., and you're impeding the treatment of this patient. I need to get Tabitha stabilized. If you don't leave, I *will* have security remove you."

Amara knew that despite their differences, Eli would hate to call security on his father. She motioned for Eric, another nurse, to take her place. "Come on, Marshall. I'll show you where the waiting room is."

"I know where to go," Marshall barked, and pulled his arm from hers.

Many people responded to stress with anger. Amara had calmed hundreds of angry relatives and friends of patients over the years. Lowering her voice, she said, "Eli is one of the finest emergency room doctors in the state."

Marshall nodded but didn't say anything as he finally started walking toward the waiting room.

"I'm sure he's more than adequate. Like this hospital, really—better than most just not great."

Amara knew her mouth was hanging open, but she was stunned. *And furious.* How dare he? How could Marshall just ignore his son's accomplishments? How could he not look at Eli and see what she saw? "Why don't you respect emergency medicine?" Amara hadn't meant to ask that, but she wanted Marshall's answer. Maybe it would help her with Eli.

"Respect?" Marshall rubbed his chin as he stared at her. "What I do is like fine art, delicate, intricate, exclusive." Marshall shrugged. "Emergency medicine has its place. But it's not surgery."

She wanted to shake him. How many of Marshall's patients had been saved by an emergency room doctor or nurse first? Hundreds. They were the ones who stabilized so many of his patients, often more than once, to make sure they had a chance for a successful transplant or heart surgery. "Eli is a better doctor than you."

Amara turned on her heel before Marshall could offer a rebuttal. She didn't care if he didn't believe it. She knew it, and she'd find a way to make Eli accept that fact too. He didn't have anything to prove to his father.

Eli wiped the sweat from his brow as he watched the intensive care team race Tabitha upstairs. The mobile CT scanner had identified a clot in her brain, the reason for her stroke. She'd stabilized after Eli had ordered an injection of tissue plasminogen activator. But her recovery was still uncertain.

Eli made his way to the waiting area to find Tabitha's husband. He was stunned to see his father sitting next to the worried man. He'd assumed Marshall would have headed back to the office by now or to his own hospital. He'd never known his father to take an afternoon off.

"Sir…"

"Mark," Tabitha's husband said. "How is my wife?"

"We managed to get her stabilized, Mark."

The man's gaze shifted between Eli and Marshall. "What does that mean?"

Eli hated this part. There was never a good way to tell someone that their life was changing. Even if their loved one recovered. "They're running some tests now. Your wife had at least one stroke."

Mark's eyes filled with tears. "But she is going to be okay, right?"

"Of course," Marshall stated.

What was his father doing? There was no way for him to know that. "Dr. Collins, that may not be true." Marshall's eyes flashed, but Eli ignored it.

Directing his attention to Tabitha's husband, Eli started again. "She coded once today. She was breathing on her own when we transferred her upstairs, and that is excellent. But if she makes it through this, your wife will have a long recovery."

Mark flinched. "Can I see her?"

Eli nodded. "Of course. I'll have someone take you to her shortly."

Eli waited until Mark had gone before rounding on his father. "You might not like telling Tabitha's husband that she has a difficult road ahead, but it wasn't appropriate for you to say she's going to be fine. You're not her physician, and you have no idea what her medical prognosis is at the moment."

Eli was shocked by his own sharp tone. The

only other time he'd stood up to his father was when he'd chosen not to become a surgeon. Marshall hadn't spoken to him for years after that, but Eli would not allow his father to offer poor medical advice in *his* hospital. Patients deserved the truth, no matter how much it might hurt to hear. He'd have thought his father understood that.

"I hate the family and patient interaction part," Marshall grumbled. "Easier to cut out the problem and replace it than talk to the family."

Eli wanted to shake his father. The patient and their family were the reasons Eli practiced medicine. To help people live their best lives.

For a man who always told his family that it was the patient who came first, Marshall often seemed more concerned about his success rate. He just saw the problem he could fix, not the whole person.

But he saved lives too, Eli thought, *a lot of lives.*

Eli was different from his father, but their reasons for practicing medicine were the same.

Save as many people as possible.

If their approach differed, did that really matter?

"Amara told me you were a better doctor than me." Marshall's statement broke through the rapid-fire of Eli's thoughts.

Eli's soul felt a bit lighter as he continued down the hall. She'd defended him to his father.

Of course she had.

Amara had always believed in him. If he hadn't already thought she was perfect, that would have done it.

"That's absurd, of course." Marshall chuckled. "And I have the stats to prove it."

"The stats?" Eli laughed.

"I've been ranked one of the top surgeons for the last decade. The last time I checked, neither this hospital nor you have ever even been in contention."

The twinge of inadequacy Eli always felt around his father sharpened. *It didn't matter. Shouldn't matter.* Marshall was tired, frustrated and concerned about a colleague. That was why he was lashing out. Eli had dealt with this many times during his career.

"I know you're worried about Tabitha." Eli kept his voice low and controlled. He could offer his father comfort. It was what he did every day of his working life.

His father's eyes shifted, and he sighed. "She's worked for me for a long time." Marshall's eyes swept over Eli. And for the first time in forever, Marshall really seemed to see him. "You did a nice job tonight. You might make that list one day too."

The tiny compliment struck him, and Eli hated that he couldn't stop his smile. Marshall hadn't complimented his career in any way since he'd gone into emergency medicine. What would he think if Eli managed to get Boston General in that report?

He'd have to respect him then.

"Eli?" Amara's voice carried down the hall.

He walked up to her and pulled her into a deep hug. "Thank you."

"For?" Amara's eyes slid to Marshall as he exited the hospital.

"For believing in me and telling my father I was a better doctor than him. It's a bit of a stretch, but I appreciate it." Eli hadn't meant to say it was a stretch out loud. But he couldn't withdraw it now.

Amara frowned. "I don't think it's a stretch."

No, she probably didn't. And that shot of acceptance made Eli feel so alive. "Amara, I—"

"Dr. Collins, there you are!" One of the med techs rushed toward them. "Dr. Stanfred asked if you'd take the elderly woman in room 2." The tech was gone before Eli could answer.

"Duty calls—again," Eli stated. "It's going to be one of those nights."

An older woman was clutching a man's arm and clearly in pain as he tried to help her walk from the bathroom to the bed in room 7. Amara and Eli raced for the couple. As Amara got her arm under the woman's shoulder, she was struck by the heat radiating off her chest. Eli's glance told her that he felt the same thing. The woman was burning up.

"What seems to be the problem?" Eli's voice was steady, comforting, as he helped the woman settle into the bed. Amara had meant what she'd told Marshall. Eli was an excellent doctor, calm in emergency situations, reassuring with his patients, always in control.

And Amara thought Marshall knew it too. Was maybe even a bit jealous of his son. Not that he'd ever admit it.

"I think my surgical incisions are infected." The woman's voice was ragged.

"Betty won't let me see," her husband added as he held his wife's hand. "But she has a fever, and she's changed her surgical dressings three times today."

"I—I—" Her throat was choked with tears as she looked from her husband to Amara. "I look so different, Harry."

"It doesn't matter, sweetheart. I love you." Harry stroked his wife's arm. "In sickness and health, remember."

Amara recognized the woman's meaning. "When was your mastectomy?" She ignored the tilt of Eli's head as she grabbed a pair of gloves and moved toward the bed.

"Two weeks ago."

She would always look different—Amara knew that. But judging her body two weeks post-surgery wasn't fair either.

"We need to look at the incisions, Betty." Eli's concerned tone raked over Amara. "I promise they're not nearly as bad as you think."

The kind statement sent a wave of hope pulsing through Amara. She patted her arm. "I know it's scary, but it *does* get better."

Eli's gaze flicked from Betty to Amara.

Would Eli tell her that her scars weren't that bad too?

Amara pushed the thought away as she looked at Betty. "In a few months, the scars will start to lighten. I promise. They go from red to pink, and eventually, they just become part of you."

"And you're beautiful, no matter what," Harry insisted as he stared at his wife. "But if you want me to leave the room, I will."

"Stay." Betty's chin wobbled, but she started to unbutton her shirt.

The redness along the scars sent a shiver through Amara. Betty needed intravenous antibiotics to get the infection under control before it spread.

As Eli explained that they needed to admit Betty for a day or so, Amara slipped from the room. She needed to get Betty's transfer paperwork done, so they could free up the room, but she had to get away from Eli too.

Every doctor and nurse knew that the scars would lighten, but by the look on his face when she'd explained that to Betty, Eli had known Amara was speaking from experience.

She was almost certain.

It didn't matter; she'd already decided to tell

him. *Show him.* And he'd been kind and supportive of Betty. It was going to be fine...*it was.*

So why were her hands shaking?

CHAPTER EIGHT

ELI SAW AMARA start to climb his steps carrying bags of groceries and rushed to open the door. "Why didn't you beep the horn or let me know you needed help with a mountain of vegetables?" he asked as he grabbed two of the sacks from her hands.

Amara had disappeared after they'd worked together on Betty last night. Her response to their teenage patient Hannah's fear that her boyfriend would dump her over a scar, and her reaction to Betty made him almost certain that she'd also had surgery, likely a mastectomy. But he was worried that if he asked, she'd shut him out. Amara was beautiful, every inch of her. Nothing could change that.

The procedure she'd had didn't matter to Eli. But it had obviously mattered to someone else. And he hated that she'd been hurt.

His phone buzzed, and he barely controlled the urge to roll his eyes or answer immediately. Part of him wanted to be able to do both. Marshall had texted about The Collins Research Group all morning and called twice this afternoon. Amara was here, so Eli silenced the alerts from Marshall.

Tonight was all about Amara, Eli reminded himself. If their second chance was going to succeed, any work needed to be on mute when he was with her.

"It's okay if you need to answer that." Amara kissed his cheek as she put a few things in the fridge. "I know your work is important."

Her offer was sweet, but Eli shook his head. "Lizzy is staying with my mom, so all we have on the agenda tonight is cooking."

"That's all?" Amara's eyes widened.

Eli stepped next to her and ran a finger down her cheek. "We can do whatever you want, Amara. Anything or nothing."

"Eli…" She suddenly closed the distance between them.

He captured her lips and felt her body mold against his. Her arms wrapped around him as her lips parted. The world righted when Amara was in his life.

Eli lifted her onto the counter, and his heart

raced as her legs wrapped around his waist. He let his fingers run through her long dark hair. He'd come to life the first time they'd kissed. Spending time with her now was heaven. Her fingers sent flames of longing running down his spine as she held him.

The oven dinged to indicate it was up to temperature, and she pulled away. "If we are going to eat dinner, I should…" Her fingers brushed her swollen lips as she gestured to the bags of groceries.

Eli pressed his head against her forehead. "Or we could order a pizza and cook tomorrow?"

Amara stared at him. "I…" She wanted to agree so badly. She'd hidden last night after treating Betty because she hadn't wanted to have this conversation at the hospital. Hadn't wanted to have it all, but if he couldn't accept her as she was, then it was better to know now. Actually, it would have been better to know weeks ago before she'd gotten close to him again. But Amara couldn't change that now.

"Pizza." Amara wrapped her arms around Eli's neck, and before she could get another word out, he kissed her. She wanted to kiss him forever, wanted to stay in his arms now and always, but he had to know.

"Eli," Amara murmured as she pulled back. His eyes were dilated with passion and need. She swallowed the last bit of her anxiety. Amara had to trust him.

Eli's fingers traced along the edge of her thigh as he watched her. "Amara, I want you. Need you, but if you aren't ready, I will wait as long as you want."

She took a deep breath. "I don't look the same." Her whispered words echoed across the kitchen. "I…" Amara paused, suddenly feeling sick.

"Had a mastectomy?" Eli asked as he kissed her forehead.

She blinked as he traced her jaw with his thumb. Sparks of need and hope lit up her body. "How do you know?"

"I wasn't completely sure, but you pull away any time my fingers move toward your breasts. You couldn't tell Hannah that her boyfriend wouldn't dump her over her scar, and you talked to Betty with such understanding."

She didn't think the look of desire in Eli's eyes had changed, but he hadn't seen the actual scars—yet. "I had a preventative double mastectomy three years ago. I took the genetic test after Mom was diagnosed. I was BRAC1 positive. I'm sorry I didn't tell you. My surgeon did a great job on the reconstruction, but… I was worried that it would…" Amara's voice died away as she stared at him. She didn't know what else to say, so she closed her eyes and waited.

His heart melted as her bottom lip quivered. "Amara, look at me." Eli kissed her cheek then waited for her to open her eyes. "You are gorgeous."

"I wanted to tell you weeks ago," she stated. "I kept meaning to. But I was scared it would make you look at me differently." Her voice quavered.

So other men hadn't been able to see past the scars. He hated that. Placing his palms against her cheeks, Eli kissed her deeply. "You are perfection."

Once again, her legs wrapped around his waist. But she folded her hands across her lap, looking everywhere but at him. "Not exactly perfection. The scars are lighter now, but…" Amara shrugged.

"Can I see them?" Eli asked. Until he saw them, she'd worry. And whatever they looked like—he didn't care. Amara was here, with him. Nothing else mattered.

Amara hesitated, then she started to unbutton her blouse. His body raced with desire as she slid the shirt off her shoulders.

She was so lovely.

Eli didn't say anything. He let his hands rest on her knees. He couldn't imagine the emotions rolling through her right now, but Eli could see what a struggle this was.

Her hands shook as she reached to unclasp her silky blue bra.

"Let me." Eli kissed the top of her ear. "You are so beautiful."

"You don't know that."

Eli unclasped her bra and slowly slid it down her arms, but never broke her gaze. Then he deliberately dropped his eyes to her chest.

"Amara." He ran his hands along the edges of her breasts, noticing each place where her breath hitched. "Your scars don't define you, love." Her lip trembled, but he didn't stop. He was not going to let her doubt how much she turned him on. "They show the strength you have, and that makes them part of the tapestry of your beauty."

Stepping back, Eli held her hands as he stared

at her, all of her. The long reconstructive scars across each breast didn't diminish her at all. He couldn't imagine the strength it had taken to make that choice. She was amazing.

"You are kind, intelligent, sweet and damn sexy." Eli held his breath as the ghost of a smile tripped along her lips.

"Sexy?" Her eyes held his. Hope hovered there, but Eli also saw the worry.

"Unbelievably so. Come to bed with me, and I will spend the rest of tonight showing you exactly how much you—*all of you*—turns me on." As soon as she nodded, Eli picked her up. Tonight, Amara was going to have no doubt just how much Eli wanted her.

And only her.

Eli's strong hands laid her on the bed, and Amara tried to calm her mind. He'd looked at the long scars, kissed her and told her how beautiful she was. Amara hadn't realized how much she needed to hear those words until Eli spoke them. She wanted to remember everything about tonight.

Eli's fingers ran along the top of her blue jeans, and she sucked in a breath as he undid the buttons and slid them down her hips. She was suddenly acutely aware that she was nearly naked, and Eli had yet to shed a stitch of clothing. He pulled away as she reached for his shirt. Self-consciousness flashed across her body. "Eli?"

"If I start stripping, I don't trust myself to savor tonight." His fingers traced lines of fire along her bare skin. "I've dreamed of touching you again for years, honey. Tonight, I'm going to worship every inch of you."

"That is quite the promise." Amara sighed as he stroked the inside of her thighs. Shivers of delight erupted along her body as his lips glided along her belly. Need poured through her as the stubble on Eli's jaw raked along her sensitive skin. She'd imagined being in his arms for weeks—years. Amara wasn't sure she could stand being worshipped. She needed him…now.

Eli kissed the base of one breast, and Amara gripped the sheets.

She could do this.

The scars were just scars. They didn't matter to him.

He paused. Raising his head, Eli trailed kisses along the edge of her jaw while his fingers moved over the scars on her breasts. "Honey, every inch of you is gorgeous to me—*every single inch.*"

Drawing a breath, Amara released her grip. She didn't have much feeling in her chest. More ghost sensations, but with each of Eli's gentle strokes, her body burned. "Eli." her voice shook as she delicately kissed his lips.

"I…" Under his watchful eyes, she grew bold. There was no room for doubt when she was in Eli's bed.

Grabbing his hand, she guided it lower. "I want you here." Her breath caught as Eli's fingers slid under her cotton panties.

His thumb stroked her as his lips traced the outer edges of her breasts, where the sensation was still the strongest. Each caress sent her soaring a bit higher as Eli worshipped her.

Cool air hit her bottom, and Amara shuddered as Eli trailed kisses lower. His tongue licked the sensitive skin along her upper thighs. She was heady with need as Eli slowly made his way to where she wanted him. Her back arched as his tongue darted across her most sensitive spot. The sensation was too much and not enough. "Eli!"

"You still taste sweet." Eli gripped her buttocks and held her as he drove her closer to pleasure's edge.

When Amara grabbed the sheets this time, it was with need. "Eli!" she moaned as he slipped a long finger into her. He stroked her slowly as he feathered kisses where they were most needed. Energy spread through her, as Amara finally gave herself over to pleasure.

Amara's release nearly sent Eli over the edge himself. Dropping his clothes to the floor, he slid back into bed with her. Tracing his hand along her hip, Eli swept a line of kisses along her shoulder.

Amara's delicate touch sent a scorching line of need across Eli's soul. Her fingers slid slowly up his back, raced across his stomach, caressed his chest as if she was trying to memorize him too.

Capturing her mouth, Eli drank her in. "Amara..." Her name fell from his lips. He doubted that heaven could be any sweeter than this.

"Eli, worship me later," she gasped. "I need you." Her hand stroked his shaft. "All of you—now!"

The demand sent his heart soaring. *Amara...*

Grabbing a condom from the nightstand, he quickly sheathed himself. Amara's lips pressed against his collarbone as he slowly entered her.

His body screamed with desire, but Eli was determined not to rush this. He'd waited too long for her. Dropping his head, he placed deliberate kisses along the base of Amara's neck as she wrapped her legs around his waist. Pulling him closer, deeper.

Drawing his lips to hers, Amara met each of his strokes. Nipping at his ear, she ran her nails lightly across his back. "Eli…" she moaned as her body convulsed around him.

Her next climax undid him. Eli drove into her. Amara gripped his shoulders, holding him, loving him. As his name fell from her lips, he let himself crest over the edge into release.

Eli relished the tender moments afterward, as their bodies lay tangled together. Home, she was home.

His Amara.

Rising, he quickly disposed of the condom and then rejoined her in bed. Running his fingers along her stomach, he cradled her beside him. Amara, in his arms, was the definition of heaven.

CHAPTER NINE

ELI WANDERED OVER to the nurses' station and handed Amara a cup of tea. Her smile sent a thrill through him.

"And here I was afraid you might stop bringing me tea, once we'd been dating a bit." Amara winked as she took a long sip.

"Was that an option?" Eli teased as she rolled her eyes. "I missed you last night." Her dark eyes caught his, and he felt like the luckiest man in the world. Amara was working beside him, staying at his place at least a few times a week and generally just making everything better in his world.

The radio by Amara's hand crackled to life. "Boston Gen.," she answered. "Repeat. Over."

"Male, midthirties, car accident. Inbound in three. Over."

Amara stood and followed Eli toward the door. "It doesn't sound critical." She moved, rubbing the back of her foot with her ankle and crossed her arms.

Preparing.

Eli nodded as he stood in the ambulance bay with her. Preparing was what emergency personnel did. Prepare for the worst, hope for the best. The paramedics hadn't indicated critical, but he'd seen minor injuries turn life-threatening in minutes.

Seconds changed lives.

A young woman climbed out of the ambulance and lost her balance. She caught herself on the door and frowned. "Sorry." She stepped to the side as the paramedics lowered a man from the back.

"Julian. I'm here." She followed a few feet behind the gurney as they walked toward trauma room 3.

"Crashed into the side of a tree. Driver's side door crushed against his shoulder," the paramedic stated as he walked beside the bed.

"The roads are wet," Julian explained, but Eli kept his focus on the paramedic.

"Airbag deployed, burns on the wrist and he hit his head." The paramedic checked a few items on the paperwork before handing it to the admitting nurse.

"This feels like an overreaction," the patient

complained as he pulled at the collar around his neck.

"Julian, let them look you over." The tall blonde slid into a chair and closed her eyes. "It will make me feel better."

"Were you in the car too?" Amara moved toward the woman.

"Passenger side. No damage. My husband, though…" The woman's words died away.

A look of concern crossed Amara's face as she caught Eli's gaze. He raised a brow, and she nodded toward the passenger and tapped her own head. "Can you tell me your name?" Amara asked.

"Kelly." The woman's voice was quiet.

Turning to Julian, Eli ran through his concussion protocols as Amara did with Kelly. Julian had a minor concussion, and his burns from the airbag were superficial. Overall the man was going to need to take it easy for a few days, but then he'd be fine.

"Eli!"

He hit the alarm by Julian's bed before racing to Amara's aid. Eli barely managed to help Amara catch the woman as she fell out of the chair.

"Kelly!" Julian yelled and started to sit up.

"I need you to stay where you are until I clear you," Eli ordered.

"My wife…"

"I understand, but stay there. Please." Eli wished there was a way to alleviate the man's panic. But Julian had a minor brain injury. The last thing they needed was two patients on the floor.

Griffin and Susan were by their sides in a matter of moments.

"She almost fell getting out of the ambulance with her husband. Her movements were slow and exaggerated, and I think the lights in here caused her pain, though she didn't tell me." Amara recited the issues as they led Kelly into her own room.

Eli rubbed the back of his neck as he walked toward Julian's room. His wife's CT scan had come back indicating a crack on the right side of her head. She'd probably hit the window, and the small bleed hadn't impacted her for over an hour.

Amara staying by Kelly's side while he examined Julian had kept the woman from further injuring herself. Amara's instincts had been spot-on. Working with her, being beside her, made every day better.

Julian needed to be careful, but they were going to release him so he could go upstairs with his wife.

"It happened so fast." He heard Julian's voice echo through the open door. "The road was slick. Kelly seemed fine. The paramedics looked her over at the scene."

"The symptoms with a brain bleed can be difficult to spot immediately. But your wife has some of the finest physicians in Boston watching over her," Amara responded. Of course, she'd checked in on Julian when their shifts ended. It was what Eli was about to do.

Eli saw Julian lay a hand across his head. "Last time I checked, I was at Boston Gen., not Massachusetts Research." Julian stopped. "Sorry, no offense meant."

He saw Amara offer Julian a patient smile. "I used to work at Massachusetts Research. If you need open-heart surgery or orthopedic care, there is no better place in the state, maybe the country." She stood and patted the side of Julian's bed. "But this *is* the top ER in the city. The staff here handle more trauma cases than any other. We just don't advertise it as well as the other hospitals." Amara winked. "Too busy focusing on our patients. Get some rest."

Eli stepped into the room. "I've come to spring you." He gazed at Amara. Every word she'd spoken had been true. This was the best ER in the city, and they *should* do a better job of advertising that fact. "You need to be careful, monitor any headaches, and if you have family nearby, it would be helpful if someone could stay with you while your wife is here."

"Thank you," Julian murmured.

"Someone will be in with your discharge paperwork shortly." Eli motioned for Amara to follow him. "You're extraordinary." He leaned as close as was professionally acceptable, enjoying the grin twitching on her lips. He didn't think he could ever tire of seeing her happy.

"Thank you." Amara gripped his hand briefly. "We make a great team."

We do.

"And you gave me the best idea for raising Boston Gen.'s profile. We need an advertising campaign highlighting the work here."

Amara blinked a few times. "Eli, that isn't your

job. Focus on the patients. Boston Gen. does great work. That's all that matters."

"We do exceptional work. And that should be publicly recognized." Eli folded his arms.

Why didn't she see that?

"It *is* recognized." Amara shrugged. "Maybe not by national magazines, where most of the votes are bought with fancy dinners, tours and things that have nothing to do with patient care. Where did the paramedics bring Julian and his wife? Here. You, Griffin, Dr. Jackson and Dr. Carmichael each get asked to give presentations at conferences every year. You were the keynote speaker at two separate conferences last year. Recognition comes in many forms. The most important kind doesn't have a trophy."

"And that is?" Eli raised an eyebrow.

She laid a hand on his arm. "The recognition that you are enough. The only person that can give that to you is yourself. But—" Amara gave him a pointed look "—there are no fancy banners that come with it."

She looked down the hall and placed a quick peck on his cheek. "I know you want this place to be nationally ranked. Want people to identify us as a first-class institution—but we already are that. We just need to fix our staff retention issues," Amara said as she headed back to the nurses' station.

Eli looked around the halls. He'd loved Boston Gen. since the day he'd walked in. Amara was right—this was a first-class ER. But she was also wrong about the rankings. What people thought, or believed, was important too. And ratings affected that. It helped with funding and would solve at least some of the retention issues. Eli was going to find a way to make sure everyone else knew how great *his* hospital was.

Amara grabbed Lizzy's cup of milk and looked toward the stairs. Eli was going over a stack of papers that Marshall had dropped off last night. Eli had promised to come down for breakfast. If he wasn't down here in a few minutes, Amara would go looking for him. She frowned.

Over the last week, there hadn't been a single day when Eli hadn't gotten a request from Marshall or worked on some project for Boston Gen. He was burning his candle at both ends and down the center. He surely couldn't keep this pace up. At least she was in charge of the health fair booth.

He trusted her with the booth, though he was still joking with Griffin that they were going to win the extra vacation days. Amara's focus was on providing good information, not winning. Cooking her mother's dishes had brought her a sense of peace. In the kitchen, cutting up vegetables, prepping the recipes, she felt closer to her mom than she had in years. Amara hadn't bought a bag of salad on any of her grocery runs this week—and she wasn't going to.

Her mother would have loved having her recipes tasted by hundreds of people. If only a few visitors to the booth made her food afterward, that would be enough. This felt like a beautiful way to honor her mom.

Lizzy laughed as she tried to pick up Amara's bag. Amara walked over and grabbed her. She'd spent the last three nights at Eli's, and she needed to run back to her apartment today. At least to get her mail and pick up a few more clothes before coming home.

Home.

Amara's feet faltered as the word struck her. Her apartment had never really felt like home. It was just a place she'd picked when her life had fallen apart. The rent had been in her price range, and Amara hadn't even bothered to re-decorate the place to her taste. But here she felt different. *Loved...*

She hadn't worked up the courage to say those words to him. Amara loved Eli; a part of her had never stopped. But she couldn't help still worrying that he might drift away. He hadn't said that he loved her either. She looked toward the stairs and wondered again where he was.

She bit her lip and tried to ignore the tiny remnant of fear pressing against her. Eli wasn't her father, and he wasn't Marshall, but what if he always persisted in chasing this dream of seeing his hospital on the national rankings—*his own name, too*?

No! She was not going to let fear of what-if stop her from enjoying the here and now. Amara had spent years away from the one person who'd looked at her and seen Amara, no matter what. That was precious. She could share his attention with his work—all his work. And whatever accolades came his way.

But their second chance still felt so new to utter the words "I love you." They had all the time they needed to get to that place. Now, if he would just come down for breakfast. As she stepped away from the counter, Eli walked into the kitchen.

"I was starting to worry you were going to spend the day in your study." Amara gave him a little finger wag.

"It's only been an hour." Eli tapped his watch as he bent to kiss the top of Lizzy's head. Then he gave Amara a much longer kiss.

His hand was warm against her back, and Amara couldn't think of a better way to start her day. "Well, an hour is a long time." She gave him another kiss before he released her.

"My apologies." Eli laughed. "You look beautiful this morning."

Amara picked up her teacup. "What is your father having you work on?"

"The Collins Research Fundraiser." Eli poured coffee into a mug and took a sip. "Guess he's been more impressed by my help than I thought."

"Well, you *are* very impressive." Amara squeezed his hand. She wished Eli didn't need to constantly prove himself to Marshall, but she was determined to tell him how proud she was of him, as often as possible. Maybe then, Marshall's opinion wouldn't carry so much weight. "Time for some breakfast."

Eli set down his mug before picking up Lizzy, taking a seat at the table and settling her in his lap. He shifted a few cut-up grapes around on the plate in front of him. "I admit that I thought he was kidding at first. He never let Sam and me help before."

"Did you want to?" Amara asked. He'd always complained about the fundraiser in the past. She'd thought he hated it.

"No." Eli shook his head, but his eyes gleamed. "But this year Boston Gen. is the focus."

Lizzy looked at Eli and popped a cut-up grape into her mouth, laughing as it squished between her lips. When he didn't react, she frowned.

To distract her, Amara sat down, then lightly bopped Lizzy on the nose before popping one of the grapes in her own mouth. Lizzy's peal of laughter echoed throughout the kitchen, and the toddler focused on making faces at Amara.

"Really, Marshall chose Boston General?" Amara was stunned.

What did Marshall want in exchange for such a prize?

Amara hated the unkind thought, but it wouldn't stop hammering inside her head.

Eli's eyes shone with excitement, and Amara

tried to ignore the twinge of unease she felt. It would be fine. *It would.* Eli was committed to Boston General, and he'd been a physician for years—he wouldn't consider an unwanted surgical residency just because his father demanded it of him.

Amara pushed the past away. Swallowing, she tried to keep her voice level. "Has Marshall ever chosen a local hospital before?" Amara guessed the answer, so she wasn't surprised when Eli shook his head.

"Which is why this needs to be perfect. If Boston Gen. can get a large cash infusion, think of all the hospital can do. We can highlight everything it does well, maybe get on that national ranking list." Eli pushed a hand through his hair.

Amara shook her head. "You don't even know the criteria for that list, and this is a fundraiser. It has nothing to do with patient care," she countered. When Eli shrugged, the touch of worry grew in her heart. Marshall was dangling a huge prize in front of his son. Acceptance.

Or the illusion of it...

Ignoring the wave of panic washing over her, Amara tried to focus on the positive. "Will our hospital get much from the fundraiser?" She put a few more pieces of grapes on Lizzy's plate. She might just squish them, but at least it kept her occupied.

"Last year, Clean Water for All took home a little over fifteen million."

"Fifteen million?" Amara felt her eyes widen. How could anyone raise that much money, particularly with one event?

Eli's eyes were bright as he took a bite of his muffin. "The lowest amount Marshall ever managed to raise with the event was just under ten million. I bet we can break the record this year. Marshall told me to shoot for twenty million."

Told him?

Amara tried to focus on the positives. With an additional twenty million dollars, Boston Gen. could fund several new projects.

"I spent this morning writing up a list of sponsors to contact and investors to reach out to. Marshall's always focused on the East Coast, but there are some new medical start-ups in California and one in Nevada that are doing some amazing things too." Eli was thrilled.

"How much of this event did Marshall turn over to you?" Amara asked, dreading the answer.

"He said I could run it." His grin sent a shiver

down her spine. "We could make a real difference." He took out his phone and started typing furiously.

"*If* you do this and Marshall still doesn't respect you, what will you do?" She kept her voice level. She hated asking the question, but she needed to know the answer.

Eli's brows furrowed, and he let out a deep breath. "But surely he would…" He paused and closed his eyes.

"He might not." Amara's stomach clenched as she watched Eli shoulders tense. He'd always wanted Marshall's acceptance. But he had to understand that his father might not ever give it—he might not be able to. Maybe it wasn't fair to push this, but even though the fundraiser was months away, this project would steal away Eli's time.

All of it, if Marshall had his way.

"Then I'll try again next year." Eli shrugged. "Marshall will eventually…" He clamped down on whatever he was going to say.

But Amara understood, and frustration rippled through her. Taking a deep breath, she reined in her emotions. "Are you going to work for Marshall full-time then?" Amara knew the answer to that, but she wanted Eli to say it out loud.

"No."

"So, you'll still have your work at the hospital." Amara swallowed as Eli nodded. "What about Lizzy? What about me? What happens to us, if you spend the next eight months spending the very little free time you already have proving to Marshall that you can host a great fundraiser? Something you didn't ask for. What do you get?"

And what do you risk losing?

She didn't say those words, though. Amara had thrown down that gauntlet years ago, and he'd let her walk away. She'd let her fear that he'd work so much that he forgot his family rule her. Eli had needed to be challenged back then just like she was doing now, but walking away without giving him a chance to think about it and change his mind had been wrong.

And cost them both.

She wouldn't do that again. Eli had promised her he could balance his work and home lives, and Amara would help him do it. *She would.* Even if that meant forcing him to acknowledge that his father might be using him.

"You're right," he said quietly. "Marshall might

never see me as an equal—probably won't." Eli's hands shook, and Amara's heart broke for him. "And I never wanted to run the whole fundraiser. I can help him smooth a few things out, but…" Eli smiled, but it didn't reach his eyes.

If only she could wave a magic wand to make Marshall see the man she saw. "You are more than enough for Lizzy and me, Eli. No matter what the rankings say, or your father thinks. You are extraordinary."

Eli gripped her hand. "That's all that matters." He kissed her cheek, but his shoulders didn't relax.

She wasn't sure he really believed her, but Amara didn't know what else to say. She slipped an arm around Eli and held him, trying to let all her feelings flow into him.

You are enough… I love you…

Amara leaned her head against the tile as the hot water slid over her skin. Her relationship with Eli was going to work this time. She wanted so badly to believe that, but the despair in his eyes racked her with guilt. Maybe she shouldn't have said anything. But what if Marshall never came to his senses? And what if Eli continued to chase after him?

Her father hadn't even called her since he remarried. It hurt, but Amara knew her father wasn't going to change. Amara doubted Marshall could really change either.

Sighing, she slid her hand along the side of her breast and performed her regular check. She'd gotten into the habit during nursing school. If she was going to remind women to check their breasts every month, Amara felt she should do the same. Now she followed the instructions her breast surgeon had given her after her double mastectomy. Even though her surgeon had done her best to get all the breast tissue, there was a small possibility with skin-sparring mastectomies for a bit of residual breast tissue to remain.

Her routine was interrupted as a small lump ran under her fingers. Taking a deep breath, Amara washed her hair and forced herself to finish her shower. She might have imagined it, or maybe there was a bit of scar tissue she hadn't noticed previously. Before shutting off the water, she performed the self-check again. The pea-size lump was still there in the same spot.

Her body was numb as she turned the water

off and wrapped the towel around herself. She'd done everything her genetic counselor, ob-gyn and plastic surgeon had recommended. *Everything.* And still there was something there.

She tried to convince herself that it was just a cyst or scar tissue as she pulled a brush through her hair. Amara stared at the clothes she'd laid out on the bed. Just getting dressed suddenly seemed like too much effort.

What if she had...?

Amara couldn't bring herself to even think the word.

Bowing her head, she dialed Susan's number. Amara wouldn't be able to focus on her patients tonight, and a distracted nurse was dangerous. Susan answered on the third ring. Amara choked out an excuse about not feeling well, which wasn't really a lie. Susan wished her well before hustling off the phone to find a replacement.

Leaning her head against the wall, Amara called her doctor. She was lucky; another patient had canceled, and they could fit her in tomorrow afternoon. Twenty-four hours and then more waiting.

Again, she looked at Eli's number, her finger hovering for a moment before she laid down the phone. He needed to work tonight, and she'd already upset him today. Plus she wasn't ready to verbalize her fears. It might be nothing.

It had to be nothing.

But when the tears started, Amara let them fall.

"What's up with Amara?" Griffin said, slapping Eli's shoulder.

"Why?" Eli asked, and immediately looked toward the nurses' station. She wasn't there. This morning, when she'd pressed him on the fundraiser, it had hurt to hear that she thought Marshall might never accept him.

He'd reluctantly agreed not to take over the whole fundraiser, though. Amara *was* right about that. Eli had never cared about it, and Boston General would make a good sum from it no matter what.

It was a considerable time commitment. And Eli didn't want to spend that much time away from his family.

His family.

That word sent a thrill through him. He loved Amara. Had always loved her. It was her soft voice repeating that he was enough that kept him grounded, even during the years they'd spent apart.

"She called in tonight, less than two hours before her shift." Griffin looked at his hospital-issue tablet and swiped a few times.

"Why?" Unease trickled down Eli's spine. Was she more upset than he'd realized this morning? She'd held him, reassured him. But Eli was suddenly very aware that he hadn't asked her how she was feeling. He'd been too focused on himself.

"No idea." Griffin raised an eyebrow. "Maybe Susan knows more."

Eli fell into step with the head nurse. "What's wrong with Amara?"

Susan didn't pause as she walked to the door of room 3. "Don't know. She said she wasn't well and sounded…not like herself. She was…" Susan let that thought die away, and her blue eyes tore through him. "Quiet," she finally added.

Eli pulled his cell out and dialed Amara. The phone rang twice before going to voice mail.

Maybe she was sleeping.

If she'd come down with a virus in the few hours since he'd seen her… Still, Eli couldn't shake the feeling that something was really wrong.

* * *

Eli raced up the stairs in the old luxury home that had been turned into a set of apartments. According to his phone, Amara had read each of his texts, but she hadn't responded. He needed to see her, hold her, to calm the racing thoughts streaming across his brain.

She'd called in sick and hadn't phoned him. That stung. They were supposed to be partners. True, they'd had a tense discussion, but Eli hadn't considered it a fight. Certainly not one that necessitated her staying off work. That couldn't be why she wasn't at the hospital.

Eli had run through a litany of possibilities on the short drive from Boston Gen., each making his blood run cold. Amara had to be all right.

She had to be...

She didn't answer his first knocks. Eli ran his hand through his hair. He didn't want to make a scene in the hallway, but he needed to see her. "Amara, honey. Open the door." Eli raised his voice and then knocked on the door twice more.

His cell buzzed, and he frowned at the screen—now she answered his texts! "Amara, I am not leaving, so either text me the location of the spare key or open the door." Eli knocked again. "Let me in, love. Whatever's wrong, I can help." His voice faltered as he leaned against the door. "Please…"

His phone buzzed again, and he straightened up. This was not how he wanted to communicate with the woman he loved. She just needed to answer the door.

Spare key under the green flowerpot.

Eli heaved a huge sigh of relief.

The small living room and galley kitchen were empty. The door to Amara's bedroom was closed. Pushing it open slowly, he saw her sitting in an oversize chair by the window.

"You're supposed to be at the hospital." Amara's voice was small and husky with tears.

His heart stuttered as she kept staring straight ahead. "That was nine hours ago."

What was going on?

"Susan and Griffin send their regards." Eli pressed his lips to her forehead as he slid down beside her.

He wrapped an arm around her shoulders, and they sat in silence. Eli felt her tears fall against his collar but still didn't speak. Whatever was wrong, she'd tell him when she was ready. The important thing was that Amara knew he was here. *No matter what.*

After a few minutes, he kissed her cheek and squeezed her hand. "I'm going to make you some tea." Her near-catatonic state was terrifying him.

Amara nodded as she grabbed a towel and headed to her bathroom.

Eli watched the clock. If she didn't emerge by the time her tea was ready, he was going to go and get her. He set the mug on the small counter just as Amara came out.

"Thank you, Eli." Her voice was stronger but still sounded far away. "Everything is fine."

"That is a lie." He folded his arms and looked at her. "We're a team now. Whatever's wrong, I'll help you fix it."

Tears flooded Amara's dark eyes as she lifted the mug to her lips. "You can't fix this, Eli. I… I…"

She bit her lip so hard, he feared she was tasting blood. "Amara?"

"I found a lump when I was in the shower." Her whispered words stole the air from the small kitchen.

Eli's stomach dropped, but he forced his face to

stay neutral. Amara was understandably scared, but he needed to be her rock right now. If this was more than just scar tissue, a cyst or…his brain forced the words away. *If* it was cancer, he'd break then, and not in front of her.

"Okay. Have you set up an appointment to have it checked?" Handle the issues you could first. That's what he always told his patients.

"Tomorrow…" Amara said as her fingers shook.

"All right." Eli took a deep breath. "If, and it's still a big if, it's cancer, then we will deal with it together."

"Together?" Amara picked up the mug and took a sip of her tea as her eyes watered.

"Of course." Eli put an arm around her. How could she even ask?

Because her father hadn't helped her mother.

The truth struck him like a blow.

Amara wasn't sure that he'd stay with her. He tried not to let that hurt. She would always come first with him—*in sickness and in health.* They may not have said those vows to each other, but Eli wouldn't walk away from Amara—ever.

"I just feel so hollow. So scared." Her voice wavered, and she sucked in a deep breath.

"That's to be expected." Eli pressed a kiss to her temple. "I've never lived with the fear of Damocles' sword falling." Amara's lips turned up just barely, but it gave him a bit of hope.

"Ancient Roman parables about death hanging above you? Really, Eli." Amara's dark eyes held his.

"It's the one thing I remember from your Ancient Roman History class. That and the pile of note cards you had all over the apartment. You must have studied those myths for months." Eli took the tea mug from Amara and set it on the counter before pulling her into his arms.

"It was six weeks, and keeping all those gods and goddesses straight was hard. Worst elective ever!" Amara let out a light chuckle. "How can I be laughing right now?"

"Because life can be funny and tragic at the same time. But you can't enjoy life if you're constantly worrying about what might go wrong. You'll go nuts." Eli wiped away a tear from her cheek.

Amara shook her head as she looked up at him. "My mom used to tell me that." She choked up again, and tears streamed down her cheeks.

Eli's heart broke at the loss in her eyes, and the worry that she'd face the same terrible diagnosis as her mother. Fear pressed against his belly, but Eli pushed it back. Whatever she faced, she'd face it with him. "Well, your mom was right. But no matter what, I'm sticking around. We're partners, Amara."

Eli stroked her arm as she leaned her head against his shoulder. He needed to touch her, to reinforce that he was there—and was staying. "No one gets promised tomorrow, Amara. *No one.* The best any of us can do is enjoy the present. Fill it with laughter, love and hope."

She wrapped her arms around his waist and let out a soft sigh. "Thank you, Eli. I should have called you, or at least sent a text."

"Yes, you should have," he agreed as he ran his hand along her cheek. "But I understand. Now, let's get you packed."

"Packed?" Amara blinked.

Eli felt his cheeks heat as he stared at her. He'd meant to ask it as a question. "I think you should stay with Lizzy and me for a bit, at least until after your doctors' appointments."

"Eli…"

Before she could offer any well-reasoned argument, he added, "You were already with us several nights a week. If you stay here, you're just going to worry. Besides, when raising a toddler, you're often too tired at the end of the day to think straight." Eli winked. He wanted her to stay with them...*forever.*

"Your toddler is adorable." Amara sighed.

"Yes, she is. But don't change the subject. I promise the time will fly by faster if you're with us." Eli threaded her fingers through his.

"I appreciate the offer, Eli. I do. But I can handle this myself. I can." Amara's lips trembled, but her shoulders were straight. The strength running through her was impressive, but she could lean on him too.

"I know you can," Eli stated. He thought Amara might be able to handle anything. "But you don't have to handle it alone. I'm here. Let me help." He squeezed her hand. "Please."

Amara's lips pursed, and she nodded. "Thank you."

Eli's heart soared as she started toward her bedroom. Relationships weren't just the good bits. Real relationships were built in the times like now, when tomorrow looked less than rosy. When life shifted the balance of everything, you shifted with it.

CHAPTER TEN

AMARA WAS SITTING behind the nurses' station, going over a few records, trying to focus. Her brain kept wrapping around what might happen. No matter how much she tried to calm the what-ifs. It was a mental reel that she hadn't been able to shut off for days while she waited for her test results.

At least being at Boston Gen. helped. This place was special. Time passed faster when she was here.

And sped by when she was with Eli.

She smiled as he turned the corner and offered her a short wave.

"My wife needs help!" Amara heard the scream, grabbed a pair of gloves and raced toward the emergency room entrance.

Outside, a young, heavily pregnant woman was lying across the backseat of a car, her breaths coming fast. Amara wasn't surprised when Eli arrived by her side and started putting on gloves.

"How far along is she?" Eli asked as he motioned for a gurney.

"Thirty-nine weeks. We were at the doctor's yesterday, and he told us we still had time."

"Well, babies have their own schedule," Amara stated as she bent to do an initial medical examination while Eli finished getting gloved. "What's your name?"

"Nicole."

"Well, Nicole, I'm Amara." She'd helped with a few emergency deliveries over the years. "I'm going to lift your dress and see how you're progressing, so we can let the maternity ward know. How far apart are your contractions?"

"They are…" Nicole flinched and let out a low groan.

Adrenaline spun through Amara. The baby was already crowning. "Eli!" Nicole was not even going to make it into the ER.

Amara exchanged places with Eli and headed to the other side of the car. Climbing into the backseat, Amara helped Nicole sit up a bit.

While Eli adjusted Nicole's legs, Amara looked at the frightened woman. "You need to try not to push, okay?"

"I have to," she whimpered. "I can't stop. My

body…" Nicole's words were lost as another contraction hit her.

Eli looked over his shoulder. "We can't move her. Get OB here now! The baby is coming."

"Breathe, Nicole." Amara kept her voice calm as the woman stared up at her. "You're going to be a mom soon, but right now, we need you to breathe."

"When the next contraction hits—"

Another contraction came, and Nicole pushed before Eli could finish his statement.

"You're doing great, Nicole," Eli offered encouragement.

The world disappeared around them. Eli, Nicole and Amara focused on the messy miracle of childbirth —in a less than ideal place. New life was coming, no matter the setting.

"You're almost there." Another contraction and the baby slipped into Eli's arms. The little boy started crying straight away.

Amara let out a breath she hadn't realized she was holding as Eli accepted a suction bulb from a person behind him and quickly cleared the baby's airway. *He was perfect.*

"You have a beautiful son," Eli announced.

"And you are going to have quite the story to tell."

A maternity nurse arrived and took the baby from Eli, and Dr. Mengh, the senior obstetrician, shifted places with him. "Nice job, Dr. Collins."

Amara looked over at Eli and grinned as he gave her two thumbs-up. They'd worked as the perfect team, and she couldn't stop the glow of warmth spreading across her as she stared at the small child and his mother being wheeled into the ER. *Could she have that with Eli?* For the first time in days, hope for the future replaced the dread in Amara's heart.

Eli stared at Amara through the doorway of Nicole's maternity room. Little Kellen was wrapped securely in Amara's arms. She was beautiful, and his heart felt like it might explode.

Her health was still uncertain, but Eli couldn't stop the image of her holding their own child. She'd be a wonderful mom. Amara was a natural with Lizzy. He wanted a family with her.

He wanted everything.

"There you are." Marshall suddenly popped up beside him, frowning. "Why are you in maternity?" His father motioned for Eli to follow him.

Pushing away from the door, Eli caught Amara's gaze.

You okay? she mouthed, and he nodded.

And he was.

"What do you need, Marshall?"

"I sent you a list of questions about Boston Gen. this morning for the fundraiser," Marshall stated expectantly.

Eli shook his head. "I've been at work, and those questions you asked should be directed to Human Resources anyway."

"They take days to respond." Marshall's eyes heated as he stared at Eli. "You should have been able to answer them in no time."

"Well, they're busy, and so am I." Eli shrugged. It was the truth, but it felt good to just state it. "If I have a chance, I'll look over them later."

Marshall's eyes narrowed as he looked back toward the room where Amara was. "Do you remember what I told you? You can be a great doctor…"

"But not a great spouse." Eli finished the sentence, believing that had cost him Amara years ago. But Eli wasn't sure he believed it anymore. What he did know was that he didn't want to be like his father. Angry over an unanswered email on an issue that didn't need to be handled immediately.

"I think I can do both." His father just hadn't tried hard enough. Eli could succeed where Marshall had failed.

"Something always suffers," Marshall stated. "Ms. Patel wasn't willing to stand beside you as you chased your goals last time. Think she'll do it now?"

"Yes." Eli was surprised by his confidence Because a decade ago, Eli hadn't been chasing his own goals.

He'd been chasing Marshall's.

They were partners, cheering each other on, supporting each other. Marshall was right. That meant some things might have to suffer, but it wouldn't be Amara, Lizzy or Boston Gen.

"If you don't push yourself, you're never going to make it out of this place." Marshall folded his arms crossly.

Make it out of Boston Gen.?

His father's statement struck him. How could Marshall think he was stuck here? Boston Gen. was where he belonged. He thought he'd made that clear—except Marshall hadn't been listening.

"You're right; I do need a change." Eli let out a deep breath as a weight lifted from his chest. "I'll send a formal response to the board, but please consider this my resignation from The Collins Research Group." Amara was right, Marshall was never going to respect him, and Eli was done searching for his approval. *He was...*

Before Marshall could respond, Amara exited the room and walked toward them. "Good afternoon, Marshall."

He didn't acknowledge her as he stormed past Eli.

"Was it something I said?" Amara looked from Marshall's retreating form to Eli.

"No. It was something I said." He grinned as Amara raised an eyebrow. "I resigned from The Collins Research Group."

"What?" Amara's eyes widened as she stared at him. "Eli, are you sure?"

"Honestly? No," he admitted. "But it felt right in the moment. Still feels right." He swung an arm around Amara. "Let's go home."

Cutting up a lemon, Amara tilted her head as the tart citrus juice fell into the pan she was heating. She'd practiced each of the recipes she was making for the health fair. Tonight was lemon rice, Eli's favorite.

He'd been in good spirits since telling Marshall he wasn't going to work part-time for The Collins Research Group or serve on its board anymore. But Amara still worried that Eli might change his mind. Or doubt himself.

It had been such a sudden decision. What if he regretted it? Or felt like she'd pressured him into it? That hadn't been her intention when she'd challenged him about the fundraiser.

But what if...?

The lemon scent wafted over her, and Amara let the worry go—mostly.

She'd grown up helping her mother in the kitchen and knew these recipes by heart. As each day passed with no test results, Amara found herself yearning to talk with her. If the veil between worlds could fall for just one day...

As the scent of lemon and spice cascaded over the kitchen, Amara felt her soul relax a bit more. Her mother would have loved that she'd reconnected with Eli. She'd have cheered them on and been first in line at their health fair booth. Particularly since they were serving her recipes.

"That smells delicious," Eli stated before dropping a soft kiss on her forehead, as Lizzy waved at him from the floor. "Tell me that's lemon rice."

"Right now, it's just boiling water, lemon and spices. But yes, it will be lemon rice in about twenty minutes." A yawn stole through Amara, and she saw Eli's eyes fill with concern.

"If you need to rest," he offered, "I can order us takeout. Or we can finally fix that frozen lasagna."

"We are never going to eat that thing!" Amara laughed and then yawned again. She appreciated all of Eli's concerns. She really did, but it was just another reminder that everything might be changing before they'd properly got started on their second chance. "I'm fine. Just tired."

His arms wrapped around her waist. "Do you need anything for the booth? You don't have to handle it alone."

"I've got it," Amara promised. She didn't need help. She was fine.

"Are you—" A loud bang interrupted them, and Eli laughed. "Lizzy's a drummer."

"Yep." Amara had flipped over three pots and set them on the floor before giving Lizzy a spoon. Lifting her head, Amara kissed him. The worries that hadn't quieted in over a week almost disappeared as she stared at Eli and Lizzy.

"This was how my mother kept me occupied until I was old enough to help in the kitchen." Amara frowned as she yawned again.

"If the health fair is too much, Amara, I can help. In fact, I—"

"No!" Amara interrupted. "I'm fine." If she said it often enough, Amara hoped the mantra would be true.

Her heart raced as Eli bent and patted a few of the pots with Lizzy. This was what a perfect life looked like. Cooking, laughing and turned-over pots.

"If you need anything, will you tell me?" Eli asked before making a silly face for Lizzy.

"Of course." Amara thought her heart might explode from happiness as Lizzy grinned and handed him the spoon. Eli hit the pots, but not hard enough for Lizzy, and soon she was re-claiming her spoon.

"I guess I need my own spoon," Eli said.

His smile was contagious as he stood, and Amara let the worries slip to the back of her mind.

Amara rolled over and sighed as Eli's arm slid around her waist. Lying next to him made the late nights with little sleep pass quicker. His breath was warm against her neck as she snuggled close, enjoying the soft sighs he made. Rubbing her hand along his muscular chest, Amara placed a light kiss just above his heart.

Eli had been her rock. Whether they were at his place or Boston Gen., Eli had kept her sane over the last week and a half. He tasted every meal she'd cooked and finally thrown out the stacks of frozen dinners with more freezer burn than she'd ever seen.

When she'd held baby Kellen, Amara had caught Eli staring at her. Was he thinking about their future too? She wanted a life with him. But what if the lump she'd found was cancer?

Eli had said he'd stand by her, and she desperately wanted to believe him. But she'd helped her mother throughout her cancer battle. Amara had been stunned by the number of relationships she'd seen that hadn't survived a diagnosis and treatment. For better or worse was a nice sentiment, but in reality it wasn't always possible.

Eli was keeping himself busy since resigning from The Collins Research Group. Amara wasn't sure he knew how to be still. He'd spent all his free time investigating how to get Boston General into next year's Best Hospitals and Physicians edition of the *US News & Reports* magazine.

He'd pored over research and websites that claimed to know what was on the surveys they sent out. Eli asked her opinions and threw stats out in regular conversation, but she was terrified that this could become an obsession. *Already was.*

Worry niggled at the back of her brain, and Amara couldn't quite push it away. She shook herself. Eli had done nothing to make her doubt him. She was letting what-ifs get in the way again, but she couldn't seem to stop them late in the night when sleep eluded her.

What if Eli never found peace? What if he always chased the rankings or some other accolade to prove to himself that he was worthy? Would it be a never-ending cycle of behavior? What if nothing she, or anyone else, did filled the hole that growing up in Marshall Collins's shadow had created? What if eventually, no matter how much she loved him, Eli followed the same patterns as her father?

Amara sighed. She was looking for things to worry about besides the potential time bomb in her body. She knew it but couldn't quite manage to force her brain to be quiet. Leaning over Eli's shoulder, she glared at the clock. Just past three.

Once again, she was going to be operating on only a few hours of sleep. It wasn't ideal for the health fair, but she'd find a way to manage. Cooking all day was easier than work. And being on her feet would keep her from falling asleep.

Soft lips pressed against the base of her neck. "Trouble sleeping?" Eli's words were husky with sleep.

Amara lightly kissed his cheek. "I'm fine. Go back to sleep."

Gentle hands ran along Amara's belly. When Eli's fingers hovered just above her panty line, she let out a light groan.

"I don't think you really want me sleeping," Eli whispered against her ear as his hand slid along the side of her breast. Then he started dropping kisses across the top of her shoulder. Gently pulling the thin straps of her tank top down, he sighed as her breasts rubbed against his hard chest.

Eli had lovingly explored her body over the last few weeks, memorizing each spot where Amara responded. He used those touches with ruthless abandon now, to drive her close to the precipice of need. She arched against him, but he held her firmly in place.

Amara felt his growing need rise against her. Rubbing her hand along the ridge of his arousal, Amara let out a soft plea. "Eli, now…please."

His hands cupped her butt, before pulling her underwear off. Eli kissed her deeply while he twisted to grab a condom. Lifting her leg over his, Eli pushed against her.

"Eli," Amara cried at his maddeningly slow pace.

His lips lingered against the sensitive skin beneath her ear as his fingers pressed against her swollen bud of pleasure. "If we're up hours before everyone else, then we have no reason to rush, Amara."

He teased her with his fingers, while his lips traced tantalizing kisses along her burning skin. Each caress drove her closer to the edge, but never over it as he continued his slow pace. It was heaven, hell and everything in between.

Gripping the sides of his face, Amara placed kisses along his jaw, quivering with need as Eli slowly drove into her—it wasn't enough. Finally, she locked her leg around his waist, her body rocketing into oblivion as he slid all the way into her. "Eli…" Amara sighed as he held her tightly.

He was hers. All the worries and doubts receded into the calm night as she claimed him. For tonight that was enough.

Eli looked at the clock on the nightstand. They needed to be at the hospital in less than two hours if they wanted to have their booth prepared for the start of the health fair. That meant they needed to be up, getting Lizzy fed and ready to go to his mom's fifteen minutes ago.

But Amara looked so peaceful for the first time in over a week. Eli ran a hand over her shoulder. Her training as an ER nurse was probably the only reason she was still functioning on so little rest.

Every time her cell rang, Eli watched her tense. And every time she saw it wasn't her doctor calling with the test results, he saw fear, hope and fatigue play across her face as she made another forced joke. He couldn't take any of her worries away. Eli was completely helpless to make this better.

His phone dinged as an email popped in from one of the hospitals he'd reached out to about their national rankings. It didn't have much information, but neither had any of the others. He just needed one look at the criteria they were being judged against. Which was beginning to seem as elusive as the pot of gold at the end of a rainbow.

Figuring out how to get Boston General on the ranking list had kept his mind occupied while they'd waited for her test results. And Amara's too. She'd looked over the stats and agreed that it seemed more like a popularity contest than it should. She'd listened to his theories. And even offered a few of her own.

Doug Jenkins, the head of Boston Gen., still wasn't sold on focusing on rankings. In fact, he'd told Eli that the only metrics he cared about were shorter ER wait times, staff retention issues in the ER, and better long-term results in the oncology department. Doug didn't consider the rankings a priority compared to providing care to the local community. And he'd flat out refused to direct personnel and resources toward winning over a bunch of journalists.

But he'd agreed to look at whatever Eli found. And Eli was determined to deliver. It would help everyone see Boston Gen. for what it was—a great hospital.

Worthy of recognition.

Amara rolled over and laid her hand against his chest. Eli smiled as she let out a soft moan, she was so content. He couldn't wake her. Sliding from the bed, Eli kissed her temple, and she didn't stir. That made the choice easy. She needed to sleep more than she needed to do the health fair demonstration.

Waiting until he got downstairs, Eli grabbed his cell and placed a call. As a precaution, he'd hired Pippin Werth, one of Boston's premier chefs, the day after Amara found the lump. Eli had tried to tell her about Pippin repeatedly. But every time he'd mentioned helping with the health fair, Amara had interrupted him. And he hadn't wanted to admit that if they got bad news before the fair, she might be unable to do it.

It had felt too much like tempting fate.

Light kisses pressed against Amara's temple. "Amara, love…" The words floated just above her consciousness. Eli's fingers ran along her side, and she moaned, not ready to start the day.

How long had it been since she'd been able to sleep until the alarm went off?

Alarm...

That word finally pierced the fog, and Amara sat up. "Did I oversleep?" She rubbed her eyes and then stared at Eli, holding out a cup of tea.

"Nope. You're waking right on time."

She looked at the nightstand, but the clock was turned away from her. She shot a glance at Eli, but he didn't seem to notice. "I need to grab a folder from the office."

Lizzy wailed as Eli moved off the bed. "I put her in the Pack 'n Play while I came to wake you up. She still hates that contraption."

He'd woken Lizzy and got her ready to let Amara sleep. That was sweet, but it had to mean they needed to get moving to make it to the fair on time. "I'll get the folder if you'll tell me where it's at."

Eli hesitated for a moment, but Lizzy let out another scream.

"If one of us doesn't get down there, she is going to tip it over." It had never happened, but Amara had watched the angry toddler rock it before, trying to find its weak spots. It was only a matter of time before she figured out a way to escape.

"Top drawer on the right," Eli stated as he rushed out of the room.

Amara washed quickly, brushed her teeth, pulled her clothes on and pulled her hair into a ponytail. It was nice of Eli to let her sleep in, but she hated feeling rushed.

She hurried to his office and pulled the drawer open to grab the only file inside. The words "Pippin Werth" were scrawled across a Post-it note attached to it. Why did Eli have the name of one of the top chefs in Boston?

The clock on the wall started to chime, and Amara felt her blood chill as the clock struck nine. They'd needed to be at the hospital by seven to ensure the booth was set up. The health fair opened at nine. *Now! The fair was opening right now!*

Flipping the folder open, she stared at a check made out for more than her monthly rent to Pippen Werth. The memo section held Eli's scrawled note: *Health Fair.*

At least she knew why he hadn't bothered to wake her. Pain rippled through Amara as she struggled to catch her breath. After all the work she'd done.

Her mother's recipes... Amara felt her heart crack. *Why?*

When Susan had joked about him hiring a celebrity chef, it had seemed so ridiculous. Apparently, his promises to let her run this on her own meant nothing. Had he not trusted her to do it right?

"We need to get moving," Eli stated as Amara entered the living room.

"Why?" Amara folded her arms and leaned against the door jamb. "Pippin Werth must have the booth under control. No doubt that's what you're paying him so handsomely for."

Juggling Lizzy, her diaper bag and her favorite stuffed animal, Eli swallowed as he saw the hurt hiding behind Amara's fury. "I'm sorry."

Setting Lizzy's bag down, he handed the squirming toddler her stuffed doll and set her at his feet too. If she tried to wander, he could put her in the play yard, but he'd prefer not to have this conversation while she screamed.

"I didn't mean to hurt you, honey. You've barely slept since..." He let the words die away.

They never talked about the lump she'd found. Eli tried again. "The health fair didn't need to be one more worry for you."

"That wasn't your decision!" Amara snapped, and he saw her flinch. "*You* decided I couldn't do this? And you didn't tell me! I'm supposed to be your partner. You promised that. Or did you figure you couldn't handle it if I lost? If your famous winning streak came to an end." Her eyebrows rose, but her voice was even.

"That's not fair," Eli protested. "You were exhausted and you needed to rest." Opening his palms, he said, "Partners help."

"Partners tell each other what they are doing," Amara countered.

Pushing a hand through his hair, Eli stared at her.

She was right.

But it was fear that had driven this decision, not pride, though the results were still the same. "I should have told you. But if Dr. Henricks…" Eli let those words die away too. He was a doctor, but the word cancer still got caught in his throat.

"Yes, you should have." Amara's lip wobbled. "There were other options, Eli. I mean, we could have asked one of the other doctors to cover for us. We could have canceled or just shown up late. There are almost thirty booths this year. It would have been fine…"

"Channel 4 is covering the event." Eli hated himself as the words slipped out of his mouth. This wasn't about better coverage for Boston General. *It wasn't.*

"So, you hired a ringer to ensure that if I wasn't *perfect*, a local news channel wouldn't see one empty booth?" Amara wrapped her arms around herself.

Tears filled Amara's eyes as she stared at him, and Eli's heart broke. "I'm sorry, Amara. I should have found a way to tell you, but I tried to talk to you about it several times. You wouldn't let me help with the fair once you took this over. Other than taste-testing duties."

"Because I had it handled." Amara's shoulders shook.

"Or because you didn't want my help? Because you still think you might have to do everything by yourself eventually? That I won't follow through on my promises." He held his breath as he stared at her. He wasn't going to walk away from her. But Amara had to believe it too or their relationship was never going to work.

"I don't need to win this year. I want the fair to be successful, for Boston General, that's all. But I also needed to help you, Amara." Eli stepped toward her.

Amara's shoulders loosened, but her jaw was still tight. "This wasn't about adding to your personal stats or Boston General's?"

Personal stats.

That jab hurt.

"No." Eli wrapped his arms around her, grateful when she didn't pull away. "I've laid beside you for the last week. I know how little sleep you've gotten. I've heard you crying in the shower."

"I didn't want to upset you," Amara whispered.

Eli lifted her chin. "I can handle the upset, Amara. My feelings for you are not so fragile that they'll be broken by a few well-deserved sob-fests."

Amara's dark eyes shimmered as she squeezed him tightly. "Sorry I didn't ask for help."

"Well, we both have things we can help each other with. Deal?" Eli dropped a kiss against her cheek. Amara bit her lip as she stared at him, and worry churned in his stomach. Could she not accept his help?

"I'll try." Amara smiled, but it didn't quite reach her eyes.

Eli kissed her cheek. "I messed up. I did it because I…"

Because I love you.

Those weren't words he wanted to fling at her at the end of an argument. She might think he was just trying to distract her. "I did it because I was trying to take care of you—but it was still wrong."

The rest of the tension finally started to leak from Amara. "I know the last few days haven't been easy, or fun."

"I've been with you and Lizzy, so they've been darn near perfect." Eli meant those words. He'd loved every second she'd been with him. Even this morning's argument had brought them closer.

"When we get to the health fair, I am taking over," Amara stated. "I'm cooking my mom's recipes."

Eli agreed. "I wouldn't have it any other way."

"Eli." Amara grinned.

"What do you need me to get?" After thanking Pippin for getting everything set up and serving the first rounds of visitors, Eli had been Amara's runner for most of the day. Their supplies were nearly exhausted. There wasn't really time to run to the store to pick up anything. If they needed to shut the booth early, that was fine.

"My phone." Amara wiggled her butt and laughed. "It's been ringing for the last hour. Can you see who keeps calling?"

Sliding his hand into her back pocket, Eli grabbed the phone. Staring at the list of missed calls, he felt his heart drop. It was Saturday, but Dr. Henricks had called three times.

If he was calling on the weekend...

"Dr. Henricks?" Amara's voice was tight as she handed a sample to a customer.

Eli nodded as he stepped up to the booth. "I'll handle things here. Take as long as you need."

Amara swallowed and looked at the small line of people waiting. "I think I made enough for everyone."

"If not, I'll start a final batch. I've watched you most of the day. Pretty sure I can follow the recipes."

"And if not?" Amara pursed her lips as she passed out another sample.

"Then, everyone will get to taste what happens when Dr. Eli Collins burns a recipe," Eli said, trying to pretend that his insides weren't turning to liquid. He too was terrified of what Dr. Henricks would say, but waiting, even an hour, didn't seem possible. Amara needed to know now.

They needed to know now.

"Go," Eli insisted. "I can't mess things up here too bad."

"You'll do fine." Amara's voice wavered a bit, but he knew it wasn't because of his cooking abilities. He'd do anything to be able to take the fear away from her.

The line of people happily accepted their small cups of curry and took the packet of recipes Amara had made. All blissfully unaware of the turmoil swirling through Eli. As the final person stepped up, he turned to look for Amara. He didn't know where she'd gone, but he needed to find her. *Now.*

Eli hastily wrote out a sign and placed it in front of the cooking station, then ducked out of the tent. Amara was sitting on a bench overlooking the small garden Boston Gen. maintained. Her head was buried in her hands, and her shoulders were shaking.

God, no...

Despite the fear almost paralyzing him, Eli forced his feet to move. Amara needed him. He sat beside her and wrapped his arms around her shoulders. When she turned and pressed her lips to his, he felt the wetness along her cheeks.

Amara pulled away and smiled. "It's only scar tissue."

Eli felt his mouth fall open. Part of him had been preparing for the worst for the last ten days. He wanted to jump up, to shout with joy, to take her home and make love to her all night, to cry... All the emotions poured through him. "I... I..." Eli wiped a tear from his cheek as a chuckle escaped his lips.

"I know. Dr. Henricks apologized for scaring me. He went into the office after attending the fair and saw the results. He thought I might not want to wait until Monday to hear," Amara whispered. "I've been sitting here laughing and crying for the last few minutes. I'm just so happy."

"I love you." The words were quiet in the garden. "I never stopped loving you, Amara, and you know it wouldn't have mattered what Dr. Henricks said. I—"

Amara placed a finger against his lips. "You're rambling."

"I know. I've wanted to say those words for so long, but I probably could have planned a better time." Eli placed his head against her forehead. She was healthy and here with him.

Amara sighed as she leaned into him. "I love you too."

Eli kissed her hard, then spun her around. "Should we go finish the last bit of the fair? Or do you want to cut out early?"

Amara grabbed his hands. "Let's go finish this thing!"

CHAPTER ELEVEN

"SORRY WE LOST, ELI. Although your winning streak was bound to end eventually," Amara said as she held up her ice cream cone. After a long day behind the stove, Eli's desire for ice cream had sounded delightful.

"I did win." Eli's lips were sweet as he kissed her. "You love me. *And* I got to enjoy some amazing culinary delights. Most importantly—" he squeezed her tightly "—you're healthy. That definitely warrants an ice cream celebration."

"I love you, Eli—I may never tire of saying that." It was such a cheesy statement, but she didn't care. She loved him, and he loved her, and for once, all Amara's worries and doubts seemed to have evaporated.

"I hope you don't," Eli whispered as he closed in for another kiss.

"Dad!" A scream erupted from the front of the restaurant.

Eli pulled back, and they moved together toward the commotion. An older gentleman was lying on the floor, surrounded by people. Amara tapped the counter and forced the employee to look at her. "Call 911. Now. Tell them that a person has collapsed, and there's a doctor and nurse on-site." She waited just long enough for the teenager to nod and grab the phone before turning to another employee. "Do you have a defibrillator?"

The teen blinked at her, and Amara grabbed his shoulders. "Do you have a defibrillator?"

"I'm the manager. There's one in the back," a woman called as she raced to the rear of the restaurant, away from the chaotic scene.

"I need everyone to move back," Eli shouted before leaning over the man.

Amara moved beside him and felt for a pulse. *Nothing.* "I can't find a pulse."

"He's not breathing. I'm starting compressions," Eli stated.

Where was the defibrillator?

Amara had listened to many health professionals discuss the different public crisis situations they'd found themselves in. She'd been grateful to never have anything to add to the discussion. At the hospital, she had options for helping a patient, machines that spit out readings. Here there was nothing but their training and hope to rely on.

"Switch out with me," Eli instructed as he counted the compressions. It was standard training. If there was more than one person, it helped to rotate compressions to avoid fatigue.

"Found it!" The manager dropped beside Eli and handed him the box containing the automated external defibrillator as Amara continued compressions. "Sorry, it was plugged into a back outlet in the office. I don't know that I've seen it in years. This place is constantly putting stuff in odd places. I once found a—"

"Thank you. Can you give us a bit of room?" Eli was polite but firm. Many people got overly talkative in crisis situations. Amara had seen more than one doctor or nurse in the hospital snap at a bystander. It was a natural response to stress, but Eli just asked her to step away. His tone was kind but authoritative, and it worked.

Dust covered the top of the AED pack. Amara managed to keep herself from cringing. Would the device work? Her arms were starting to get tired, but she kept going while Eli prepped the machine. It booted up, and she saw his shoulders relax a bit. He obviously hadn't been sure it would function either.

Amara moved her arms while Eli cut the man's shirt and placed the shock pads against his chest before resuming compressions. Then she lifted her arms as the AED ordered the shock. *Please...*

The man's son let out a moan as the AED failed to register any heartbeat following the shock, and Eli took over from Amara.

She strained her ears and heard a siren in the distance. Time raced ahead as the AED set up its next charge. Following the second shock, it registered a heartbeat, and the relief among the restaurant patrons was palpable.

Amara and Eli didn't shift their positions. They needed to be ready if his heart stopped again.

When the ambulance finally screeched to a halt outside the building, Amara felt her insides begin to relax. She and Eli stepped back as the paramedics raced in. Eli quickly relayed what they'd already done before stepping away to let them work. The paramedics nodded to Amara and Eli as they prepped the man for transport to the hospital.

The man's son hurriedly offered Amara and Eli a thank-you before rushing after his father.

"You're welcome," Amara called, though she doubted he heard her.

She sighed as Eli wrapped an arm around her waist. She stared at the departing emergency vehicle as the bystanders started to go back to their seats. At least they'd been able to give the patient a chance.

"Thank goodness you and your wife were here." The manager beamed as she stepped in front of them.

The assumption surprised her, and she looked to Eli while letting out a soft giggle. Shaking her head, Amara said, "Nope. We're not married."

But maybe one day.

The thought brought another smile to her lips. Eli was the one she wanted to spend all her days with. He belonged with her.

And she with him.

"Oh." The woman looked at Eli's arm around Amara's waist and blushed. "You just work so well together. Of course, colleagues," she muttered before wandering off.

"Colleagues?" Eli laughed and shook his head. "I feel like there are half a dozen terms I'd use before that."

Amara's stomach danced as her lips touched his cheek. "Such as?"

"Let's see, partners, lovers, my…"

A young woman tapped his arm to grab Eli's attention. "You're Dr. Eli Collins, right?"

Eli nodded. "Yes. Sorry, do I know you?"

"I'm Lia Trupee, a reporter with Channel 4. I saw you at Boston Gen.'s health fair. Can you give me a brief rundown of what happened here?" The blonde nodded to Amara but kept her focus on Eli.

After giving a brief statement on the events in the restaurant and refusing to comment on the likely outcomes for the patient, Eli transitioned the conversation to some of Boston General's perks. Amara beamed as he talked about what the hospital had to offer and the expertise of its professionals. She wasn't sure Lia would use any of his additional commentary in the article, but the pride radiating off Eli was contagious.

"Look, Boston Gen. is in the paper!" Susan handed a copy to Eli and Griffin.

"I didn't realize people still bought the paper." Griffin smirked as Susan glared at him. "They do when their friends and hospital make the news," she told him.

Griffin frowned as he turned the paper over. "Do you mean the small paragraph on page six regarding Eli and Amara stabilizing a heart attack patient who didn't even arrive at our hospital afterward?"

Amara had followed up on the man they'd treated in the fast food restaurant. Mr. Thomas March was recovering well at Marshall's hospital. Eli had tried to follow up with his father too, but all Marshall had said was that the patient was in the city's *best* hands. Eli hadn't responded to the not so subtle insult.

But it still stung.

"Very funny." Susan slapped her copy of the paper against Griffin's arm. "We rarely see our hospital or its employees in the paper. Lighten up."

Eli read over the small paragraph. He knew that all his comments regarding Boston General couldn't have made it into the local paper. But it would have been nice if they had mentioned just a few of the hospital's selling points. Would it have killed the paper's bottom line to praise the hospital where the "heroic medical profession-als," of their article actually worked?

"Eli." Amara stepped beside him. "Mrs. Del-gado's daughter is here."

"Did you see the article?" Eli asked as they walked back to the room.

"I think Susan has shown it to everyone. Don't tell her, but I think 'heroic medical profession-als' is a bit much." Amara rolled her eyes before crossing her arms. "A warning—Mrs. Delgado's daughter isn't happy."

Eli paused a few steps from the door. "Why?" Dealing with difficult patients and their families was unfortunately common in the ER.

The woman's mother, Helen, had a bad chest cold, and as a precaution, she had been brought in by one of her nursing home's caregivers. Mrs. Delgado had just had her ninety-first birthday, and most of her issues were age-related. Eli had recommended rest, fluids and monitoring. He'd just started the discharge paperwork when Susan brought the newspaper over.

"Not sure. She wanted to talk to a doctor. Not just some nurse." Amara sighed, but he could see her frustration.

Nurses were the lifeblood of any unit. But

many people saw them as unimportant assistants to the doctors. He'd explained to more than one patient that he hadn't run an IV since his last year of residency, but that most of the nursing staff could do it in under a minute with their eyes shut.

"I'm sorry, Amara." She was one of the best he'd ever worked with, and it was a shame that anyone would question that.

"Thank you. But it's nothing I haven't heard before." She waved her hand. "Just annoying. By the way, the daughter's name is Sylvia Mora."

He was in awe of her as they walked into the room. Amara was certain that she was a good nurse. She never doubted that she did her job well. Never let the cutting statements of others touch her. If only Eli could figure out how to let the jabs roll off him too.

Sylvia Mora was pacing back and forth, barking into her phone. As her eyes latched on to them, she hung up without saying goodbye to whoever was on the other end. "Have you done blood work on my mother?"

The tiny woman in the bed let out a soft snore, and Eli sighed. "Your mother has a chest infection. It will clear with a few days of rest and fluids. As we age, our veins weaken. If we take her blood, which I assure you will not give us a different answer than chest infection, we run the risk of her veins blowing or collapsing. That is painful, and she'll have bruises for at least a week—probably longer. I don't want to put her through any unnecessary discomfort."

Mrs. Mora glared at him. "Have you taken a chest X-ray?"

"No. I listened to her lungs," Eli explained.

"She could have pneumonia," Mrs. Mora shouted. "And you are refusing to do your duty." Her screech echoed in the small room, and still, the woman in the bed didn't stir.

Eli took a small step toward Mrs. Mora and offered a reassuring smile. No medical intervention could stop the passage of time. But many people often weren't ready to accept the inevitable end, and Eli understood that too.

Keeping his voice level, he started, "When people hit a certain age, they're—"

"So, because she's old, you think you can be lazy. Why on earth did her nursing home bring her here? Worst hospital in Boston."

"No, it's not," Eli argued. He was stunned by how much that cut. Mrs. Mora was worried about her mother, but her perception was wrong. *Very wrong.* Boston General had some of the finest physicians and nurses he'd ever had the opportunity to serve with. Including the one standing next to him.

Amara gripped Eli's arm before addressing Mrs. Mora. "Your mother is resting comfortably, and her chest infection will clear in a few days on its own. Any other hospital would tell you the same thing."

Mrs. Mora held up her phone and started scrolling through a website. "Really, would Dr. Anderson at Massachusetts Research tell me that? She has a five-star rating on RateMyMD.com."

What was RateMyMD.com? Eli had no intention of asking Mrs. Mora that question, but he promised himself that he would investigate it later. "Yes," Eli replied, "She would tell you the same thing." He was certain of his diagnosis, and no amount of blood work or chest X-rays would change it.

Mrs. Mora turned back to her phone and furiously started typing before holding up her phone again. She grabbed her purse. "You only have three and a half stars, so you'll excuse me for wanting the best for my mother."

Three and a half stars?

Eli knew it was ridiculous to care about ratings on an internet app. It didn't mean anything, but a niggle of uncertainty bit into him.

Who had found his care lacking?

"Dr. Collins is one of the top ER professionals in the state. He speaks at conferences and is well-respected by his peers." Amara leaped to his defense, but Eli waved her down.

"Your mother's discharge papers will be ready shortly. Her chest infection *will* clear in a few days, and she'll be fine."

"You're right—she *will* be fine." Mrs. Mora picked up her purse. "Because as soon as we leave here, I'm taking her to Massachusetts Research."

Eli nodded but couldn't force out any words. If Mrs. Mora wanted to take her mother for a second opinion, that was her right. But he wanted to know what RateMyMD.com was saying about him…and Boston Gen.

"It looks like a star-based system, where patients rate their experiences," Eli stated.

Amara looked at the lines drawn across his forehead and gripped his hand. "Eli, these sites pop up and go dark all the time. It's strangers making random complaints."

Eli nodded, but he continued to flip through the reviews. "I know that, but several doctors have updated their own profiles in here to indicate they were nominated for the annual report."

If Amara could discontinue that report, she'd do it in a heartbeat. It was useless, but Eli was still obsessed with it. She frowned as he showed her the stats for two other Massachusetts Research doctors.

Grabbing his cell, Amara stared at it. "These apps don't matter." Amara read out one of Eli's five-star posts. "'Dr. Eli Collins is one of the best! He joked with my son and kept him entertained while putting a cast on his ankle.'"

Amara pulled up another.

"'Dr. Collins is responsible for my father being alive at Christmas. He realized his headache was a brain bleed.' You can't hear those words and think you aren't great."

If he wanted acceptance from strangers, why couldn't Eli focus on *these* reviews?

Eli shrugged. Pulling up a few of the one-star reviews, Amara glared at them. Most were complaints about wait times. One woman complained that the food in the cafeteria was cold. They had nothing to do with Eli. *Nothing!* "Everyone gets a bad review. It doesn't mean anything. I love you, so shall I leave you a five-star review?"

"I love you too, but if you want to leave a review…" Eli sighed as he grabbed the next chart. "I'm kidding. You're right, Amara, of course. It's just a dumb app."

Except that she wasn't sure he believed that. Or believed in himself. Eli patted her hand, and Amara wished there was some way she could silence his inner critic.

"You're right. Love you. Thank you for keeping me grounded." He smiled, but the cloud of uncertainty still hovered in his eyes.

"I think we should look at vacation spots for next year." Amara slapped an Italy tour guide on the stack of papers in Eli's lap.

He looked up as he set his papers on the coffee table.

Next year…

Those two words sent a thrill through him. "You pick the date and place, and I'll be there."

"It's more than picking a date and a place," Amara said. "Half the fun is planning the adventure. Poring over research—" she eyed his papers "—planning out schedules to see all the sights. Then ripping the schedule up and sleeping in late!"

Amara beamed. "I bought two more guidebooks today too. Figured we might want to plan based on the season. The winters in Boston can be pretty icy. Do we want to escape then? Or spend a week somewhere cool in the summer?"

"Two more?" Eli laughed, "Are we going to own every guidebook ever written?"

"Maybe." Amara tapped his nose.

Eli pulled her into his lap. His lips captured hers. He sighed as Amara's fingers ran through his hair.

"You're trying to distract me," Eli accused as Amara grinned.

"Guilty." She glared at the stack of papers next to him. "You're still wrapped up in the national rankings. You've been digging through apps, ratings and survey criteria for over a week. You even slept on the couch last night. You need a break, Eli."

"It's interesting." He kissed her, hoping it would erase the tiny downward turn of her lips. "Some people argue the rankings are the thing that defines an institution. Others claim the rankings are bought. What no one discusses is how to get on the survey. And that's the key. If you don't get on the survey…get your hospital on the survey," Eli corrected. "Then you can't be on the final list."

Eli tapped the stack of papers. "But I am going to find out. Boston General is at least going to be nominated this year."

Amara's frown deepened, and his heart clenched. He'd been so focused on these apps and ratings that he hadn't been very present this week. And that wasn't fair to his family. Eli grabbed for the guidebook in her lap. "But tonight, none of that matters, because we are talking about vacations."

Her eyes lit up as she flipped to a few pages that were already dog-eared. Her enthusiasm was contagious. It almost made Eli forget the stack of papers and research beside him.

Almost.

"Are you coming to bed, Eli?" He hadn't come up to bed with her in several nights, but she wanted to believe tonight would be different.

Please.

"What did you say?" Eli asked without looking up from the couch.

Amara was trying not to be jealous of the various papers and folders spread across the living room. It was ridiculous to compete with his research. But it was hard when those items seemed to be able to hold his attention far longer than she could.

How could this have happened so quickly? How could he slide away from her so easily? She knew this was important to him, to what he wanted for Boston General. But what if this was only the first of a lifetime of important projects?

Amara tried to push that fear aside as she watched him furiously write out notes as he scrolled through another web page. "Are you coming to bed?" she repeated.

Eli blinked as he turned to face her, and then he rubbed his eyes. He smiled and winked, but Amara saw his exhaustion. "I'll be up in ten minutes, honey. Fifteen tops."

"Promise?" Amara asked as she walked over to drop a kiss on his lips.

"I promise," Eli stated, but his eyes were already focused on the screen in front of him.

"I love you," Amara called as she started for

the door. She paused for a moment, but Eli didn't answer back. It was fine, she promised herself. But it was worry that carried her off to sleep—alone.

CHAPTER TWELVE

ELI WAS LATE for their date—again. Twisting the fork around on her plate, Amara glared at the hands on her watch. If she'd wanted to eat alone, she could have gone back to her apartment and done that.

They'd planned to meet before each of their shifts for the last week. Eli had gotten progressively later every day—at least she hadn't waited to order today. Yesterday, Eli had been so late, they hadn't managed to eat anything. She wasn't going to arrive at Boston Gen. hungry again.

Irritated but not hungry.

Boxing up the sandwich she'd ordered for Eli, Amara hated the tears hovering in her eyes and the fear that was increasingly wrapping around her heart. He was pulling away from her. Slipping into work and letting his family slide—just like her father had. What if she wasn't enough compared to apps and rankings and his desire to be the best?

Eli checked his email first thing in the morning, and it was the last thing he looked at before bed—when he made it to bed. Last night was the third time this week that she'd come downstairs to find him asleep on the couch. And it was only Wednesday. She'd woken up holding his pillow this morning, and it was a poor substitute for the man she loved.

Eli had spent weeks outlining plans, making suggestions and contacting anyone he could about getting Boston Gen. on the annual survey to determine the nominations. Even the head of their hospital was finally on board with Eli's plans. Though Amara wasn't sure that Doug really thought of it as anything more than a useful staff retention tool.

Amara thought there were better ways to recruit talented medical professionals. Over the last three months, they'd lost fewer personnel. Eli had also told her the numbers had been trending down. So the hospital had already been doing the right things.

Still, she'd tried to help, but Eli had been distant.

No, that was unfair.

He'd been focused. Amara understood his need

to prove what all the long-term employees of Boston General knew. But he'd pushed everything else aside in order to do it.

After they put Lizzy to bed, Eli spent at least a few hours going over statistics about other ERs, and how Boston Gen. was better. Or how he thought the hospital could improve.

When Amara had pointed out that her former hospital was in those rankings, and she didn't think that it had added much to the patient care, Eli pulled out an entire folder marked *Massachusetts Research*. He'd pulled papers out and gone over three years' worth of data. She didn't think he'd even heard her when she'd told him good-night and finally gone to bed.

Alone—again.

Her lip trembled as she stepped from the small sub shop into the afternoon heat. Checking her phone one last time, she sighed at the lack of text messages and voice mails. Eli wasn't coming.

He'd promised her balance, and for a while he'd delivered. Though for the last few weeks, while his body had been present, his mind had been elsewhere. Maybe she'd been kidding herself that they could have a future together. If someone you loved was so easy to forget…

"Amara!" Eli's voice was ragged as he ran toward her. "I'm so sorry!"

Her heart clenched as she stared at him. Trying to lock her hurt away, she took a deep breath. Maybe there was a good reason this time.

Eli dropped a swift kiss to her lips. "I lost track of time. But I found it!" Eli gripped a folder. His grin was huge, but it looked too forced. It was a look he'd worn so often since they'd found out about the RateMyMD app.

Eli's cheeks heated as his eyes cut to the box in her hand. "Any chance you ordered me a sandwich?"

Handing him the box, Amara asked, "What was so important that you missed lunch? Again."

He pulled out the sandwich out and took a giant bite. "You are the best. What would I do without you?"

You'd get by.

The phrase struck Amara's heart with a resounding crash. Without her, Eli would get by. He'd focus on Boston Gen. and Lizzy. Find a new project to tackle and be okay.

But what would she do without him?

Amara opened the folder and tried to make sense of the numbers and random pie charts on the pages. She raised an eyebrow. "What am I looking at, Eli?"

"The criteria for the annual report. Or at least part of the criteria." He took another bite of the sandwich as they walked toward the hospital.

"So, I got stood up for a bunch of graphs, charts and statistics?" Fury spun through her. He'd chosen a stack of paper over lunch with her.

"I mean, no. It's just this is what we've been looking for."

"What you've been looking for, you mean," Amara bit out.

Eli nodded, flinching as he met her angry gaze. "Yes. What I have been looking for. But it helps everyone. Ensures Boston Gen. gets the credit it deserves." He tapped the papers in the folder.

"Or the credit *you* deserve?" Amara sighed as she handed the folder back to him, suddenly too exhausted to be angry. "All this because one patient decided to take her mother to a different emergency room—for a second opinion. It was a fear-based reaction on her part, and your ratings on that app don't mean a thing."

Eli halted beside her, but Amara kept walking. They needed to get to work, and she didn't want to hear any more about stats, rankings or apps.

Not today, at least. Amara went through the ER's front doors, Eli close on her heels.

"Amara, honey, I'm sorry. I should have called."

"Yes. You should have." Amara walked into the staff lounge, pulled open her locker, deposited her purse and then faced Eli. "I know you're super focused on Boston General's rankings right now. I know you think that it is some magic pill or something, but you've become obsessed. You have to focus on other things too."

"There were two articles about our hospital in the news this week, Amara," Eli told her. "My plan is working."

"I know!" Amara slammed her locker shut and winced as the noise reverberated around the room. "I know how many articles there were. I know what our stats look like. I know what Massachusetts Research's stats look like. I know the stats for six hospitals in California because I love you and have listened to you going on about it, am still listening to you. But you promised me balance. You told me you loved me."

"I do love you," Eli insisted.

She hated feeling like an afterthought. "This week, you have been late to every date, and even when you arrive, your focus isn't on us. You stood me up today without even so much as a text message for a folder full of papers. I deserve to be remembered. To not take second place to an award." Amara bit her tongue as Griffin walked in.

"I have to do the research, Amara. It's important, so important." Eli's voice was tight as he gripped the folder.

"Research that is more important than your family? Than me?" Amara's voice was hollow as she stared at Eli. "Do you even hear yourself?" He sounded so much like Marshall and her father that Amara's heart tore.

She couldn't stay here. If she didn't leave, she was going to say something she'd regret, or start crying. Neither option would make her feel any better. "I need to get to the nurses' station." She didn't look back.

Eli leaned his head back against the lockers as Amara's words washed over him. He'd never meant to make her think that this project was more important to him than her. It wasn't. But he'd done a poor job of showing that. Eli knew he was focused, knew he seemed borderline obsessed. He didn't know how to explain the emotions rolling through him to Amara. This was a desire she couldn't understand.

After all, she never doubted that she was a good nurse. If she'd received a one-star review, she'd write it off as a disgruntled patient and move on. Eli wanted to do that, but his brain spun around the numbers and the fear that they meant he'd failed his patients. When people made comments about Boston Gen., she ignored them, secure in her knowledge that those opinions didn't matter.

But she was wrong; opinions mattered to most people. That was the argument his brain kept screaming, and rankings and awards elevated opinion. Which helped with staff recruitment, retention and fundraising. It wasn't Boston Gen.'s primary focus, but fundraising helped provide the newest technology at a lower cost. That helped their patients. After doing a bit more research, he was certain that Boston General could be considered for the list this year.

That he could be...

Amara was right, too; he hadn't been present enough lately. He'd let his need to prove that this hospital was great, to show it off to the community overtake him. Amara deserved better. He loved her, and Eli never wanted her to doubt that. He was going to make this up to her.

Amara was at the nurses' station, going over paperwork when Eli exited the staff lounge. Her eyes were hooded with exhaustion. Was she having a difficult time sleeping too? They were going to bed at different times lately. Or more accurately, he was falling asleep on the couch.

"I'm sorry I stood you up, and I am sorry that everything has been so crazy. I almost have everything under control." Eli placed a cup of herbal tea on the counter and offered her a small smile.

"Do you?" Amara blew a piece of hair away from her eyes as she stared at him. "Do you even know what you want, Eli?"

Fear slipped down his spine as she refused to acknowledge the tea. Had he done more damage than he realized? "To be recognized." Eli shook his head "For Boston Gen. to be recognized," he corrected.

"And if it's not?" Amara pressed. "What if you can't figure out how to get the hospital on the rankings list? What if they reject you for a survey?"

"Then, we keep trying," Eli stated. His stomach sank as Amara looked away.

"Amara?"

She leaned forward, her eyes clear as she met his gaze. "Eli, if you want to work at a nationally ranked institution, then maybe you should take a job at Massachusetts Research or one of the others on the list. Your résumé is impressive. I am sure any of them would be thrilled to employ you. If recognition will make you happy, will make you realize…" Her voice caught, and she swallowed hard.

Her words felt like a knife twisting through his side. This wasn't about working at a nationally ranked institution. It was about their hospital getting the recognition it already deserved. How could she not see that? He wasn't doing this for himself—well, not only for himself anyway.

"Amara, I don't want to work anywhere else. They've been calling and sending me letters for years and I've always said no." Eli looked over her shoulder at the emergency room.

This was where he was meant to be. He'd known that the first day he'd walked through the door. Boston Gen. did good work. Important work. And the doctors and nurses here deserved that recognition.

They'd earned it.

Eli was tired of explaining why he never took the positions that were offered from other hospitals. Tired of defending his ER. Tired of people disregarding it.

Amara took a folder from one of the techs and stood up. "Hospital accolades are not going to make you feel whole. And they won't matter to Marshall."

"It's not about that," Eli bit out.

"Are you sure?" Amara raised an eyebrow.

Eli wanted to say yes, but his tongue refused to produce the word.

Why was she bringing his father into this?

"Let me make today up to you. How about we go out tomorrow? A real date? I'll pick you up, and we'll go anywhere you want." Eli frowned as Amara looked at the papers in her hand instead of at him.

Her eyes were shiny when they finally met his. "I don't know, Eli." She crossed her arms. "I want you to succeed, I really do, but your family can't trail after you on the path of life."

The hurt hovering in her eyes made Eli flinch.

He'd done that—again.

Eli's chest ripped open. He couldn't lose her; he couldn't. "I love you. I do. I know things have been hectic, and I have been more than a little distracted. I promise you it won't keep happening. You and Lizzy are the most important things to me. I swear. Where do you want to go—name the place and time, and I am there. No distractions!"

Amara's teeth dug into her lip, but she nodded. "I want to go dancing. And I am going to hold you to your promise of no statistic discussions."

"Dancing?" Eli asked.

"Dancing," Amara repeated. "The two of us together, close to each other, swaying to the music." A tiny smile touched her lips as she looked at him.

Eli's heart started beating again. She wasn't walking away. He hadn't lost her. He just needed to refocus. "I'll make sure that my shoes are shined."

Big news! Can we reschedule dancing? I'll call soon.

Amara read the text and looked down at the black dress that she'd picked for this evening.

The V-neck cut was lower than anything she'd worn since her double mastectomy. But she'd gone back to her apartment tonight, pulled it out of the closet and slipped it on, excited to see Eli's reaction. If they'd gone dancing, it would have spun beautifully.

How many times had she'd seen her mother waiting on her father? Listened to the voice mail apologies that they'd need to reschedule something while he chased his dreams. Her mother always believed he'd come, but with each new round of success, his family slipped further away.

It'd started with missed dinners and dates and ended in a lifetime of loneliness. Amara couldn't do that—wouldn't. Her breath was ragged as she grabbed her keys, but she forced her feet to keep moving.

If she didn't end this now, she was worried that she'd never work up her courage again. She couldn't be an afterthought to her partner for the rest of their lives. It was better to be alone than plan events the person you loved didn't attend.

Her heart bled as she walked to her car. The tears started, but Amara didn't bother to push them away. After all, her makeup didn't need to be perfect for a night out anymore.

* * *

Eli raised a glass with Mr. Jonah Richards. The researcher responsible for sending out surveys was in his home. The surveys determined who made the US News & Reports rankings. Victory was so close.

The front door opened. "Eli?"

Eli blinked as Amara's voice carried down the hall. What was she doing here? She was supposed to be getting ready at her apartment tonight. He'd sent her a text. Told her he'd call soon. He hated that they'd had to reschedule their date, but when he explained what this meant, he was sure she'd understand. She wanted him to succeed—she'd said it herself only yesterday.

"We're in here, Amara," Eli called. "I'm glad you came. There's someone I want you to meet."

Her eyes were red from crying, and ice slid down Eli's spine. It was his fault. But there had been a good reason.

A great reason.

"This is Jonah Richards. He's responsible for the annual report." Eli smiled and tried to catch her eye.

"Well, I help organize it. We're actually starting this year's interviews and surveys next week. Very good timing on your boyfriend's part."

She crossed her arms and raised an eyebrow at Eli. "Not sure about that," Amara stated bluntly. "I just need to get a few things."

As Amara headed for the stairs, she nodded to Jonah. "Nice to meet you. For the record, I think Boston General is a wonderful place to work."

He'd hurt her—again. But Eli had gotten their hospital included in the survey. Amara would celebrate with him.

She would.

Eli's heart clenched as her tearstained face floated before his eyes.

Wouldn't she?

Eli nodded toward Jonah. "Just give me a few minutes."

Jonah's eyes had followed Amara's departure. "I need to be heading out anyway. My wife will be wondering where I am. We'll be in touch, Dr. Collins."

Eli accompanied Jonah to the door and said good-night, then hurried upstairs.

"Amara," Eli choked out as he saw her picking up her book from the nightstand and grabbing all the clothes that she'd kept here over the last month. "I'm sorry. He called and had some urgent questions. I had to—"

"I understand, Eli." Her words were barely audible.

For a moment he could breathe again. Amara understood. So why was she still packing her things? When she finally looked at him, the sorrow in her dark eyes broke him.

"I'm sorry, Amara. We can go dancing now," Eli suggested. "To celebrate! Your dress is gorgeous; you are gorgeous. I'll change right now. Lizzy's already at Mom's."

Her eyes flashed, and she shook her head. "So, you got us approved for the survey." Amara zipped up the bag and put it over her shoulder.

"Yes," Eli said, but he was suddenly terrified of what it might cost. "Please." He swallowed hard. How had he let something come before her again? *How?* "Stay."

"I want to." Amara touched his cheek. "I do."

"But you're not going to." Eli's heart was shattering as he stared at her.

Amara sighed. "I've spent the last several weeks waiting for you. Waiting for you to come to bed, only to finally sleep alone. Waiting at lunch, waiting tonight. I warned you I wouldn't compete with statistics and accolades. Tonight was supposed to be our night, ours. No matter what. You promised me. And yet—work came first."

Amara sucked in a deep breath, but she kept her eyes focused on him. "Did you consider rescheduling with Jonah? Setting up a time to see him tomorrow?"

"No." Eli realized what he had done, but he told her the truth. He'd been so excited that he'd texted the quick note to Amara and invited Jonah to his home to talk immediately. "It won't happen again."

"I want to believe that." Her voice broke, and Amara visibly tensed before continuing. "But you promised me the exact same thing yesterday. And in less than twenty-four hours, something else took priority over our plans. I want to be a partner, a wife, a mother. And I want a man who comes to bed with me, wants to raise our children together, arranges dates and then actually goes on them with me."

She added, "I want to be someone's priority. Maybe that is selfish, but I want to know that I come before a building or an organization that can't love you back."

You do. Eli wanted to scream those words, but his mouth refused to open.

Her hand laid against his cheek for just a moment longer. "I hope that one day when you look at yourself, you'll see what's really there. And I hope you accept that man whether he's won countless awards or none." Amara dropped her hand and headed for the door. "He's truly exceptional."

Eli felt his soul crack as Amara walked out the door. She'd told him what she wanted in a partner, and Eli had sworn to be that man. It had been in his grasp until he'd gotten distracted. He'd chased someone else's acceptance when he'd always had hers. She'd walked away from him—again—and he totally understood why.

Pulling out the drawer on his nightstand, Eli lifted out the small ring box. He'd chosen it weeks ago and planned to ask her... *When?* He'd been too busy to make the time.

He groaned. When he'd finally finished with his plans for Boston Gen.? He'd put off asking the love of his life to marry him because he was too busy chasing stats and interviews.

The cup of tea was still warm as Amara sat behind the desk. It didn't have a note; none of the others had either. She and Eli hadn't been on the same shift all week. He'd effectively removed himself from the schedule any time she was on it. Without the pain that still radiated through her body, Amara might believe the last few months had been the best and worst dream.

"The surveys from *US News & Reports* arrived today." Griffin laid the envelope on the nurses' station and walked away. She contemplated throwing it in the trash, but if Eli had managed to get Boston General nominated for the list, she felt honor-bound to fill out the staff survey.

"Look!" Amara heard one of the nurses let out an excited squeal. "This is so exciting."

Holding the envelope in her hand, Amara stared at the staff around her. They were all excitedly holding their surveys. Congratulations, smiles and laughter dominated the ER floor.

Over just being nominated...

Amara felt her insides chill. Eli was right— the staff had wanted that recognition. And he'd given it to them. She'd been so worried about being left behind that she hadn't considered others wanted it too.

A pit formed in her stomach as she ripped open

the envelope. Eli should be here to see the people he usually worked with celebrate. Amara's fingers were numb as she stared at the list of hospitals and practitioners. Dr. Carmichael and Griffin were both listed as potential candidates. Where was Eli's name after all the work he'd done to make this happen?

Amara marched toward Griffin, shaking the survey paperwork. "Where's Eli's name? I know the hospitals get to nominate their physicians. Where is it?"

"Is it me or Dr. Carmichael you think doesn't belong?" Griffin held up his hands as Amara glared at him.

"Eli turned down his nomination." Griffin sighed. "Happy?"

No. "He…he…" Amara felt her insides shake. *Had her fears cost Eli his dreams?*

Her heart raced as she stared at the list. She'd challenged him to put her first, but Amara hadn't meant to make him give up on the accolades completely.

Or had she?

Heat engulfed Amara's skin as she stood among the celebrating staff. Was that the only way she'd think he was putting his family first?

She wanted to say no, but the truth floored her. Had her love really been that fragile?

Amara crumpled the sheets of paper and then started straightening them out. Eli had worked hard for this. She couldn't just throw it away.

Like she'd thrown their relationship away...

Amara forced herself to breathe. Despite everything he'd done, Amara had played the what-if game and only focused on the negatives. What if this was enough for Eli? What if seeing the staff at Boston Gen. happy was all he'd really wanted? What if she'd been willing to reschedule a dancing date or waited for him to call? What if she could have had everything she wanted, and Eli could too?

Lizzy was playing on the floor while Eli downed another cup of coffee. He hadn't managed to get much sleep since Amara left. But he'd taken a cold hard look at himself, and Eli had not liked the image in the mirror.

He'd been chasing recognition for so long. First from Marshall and then from a stupid survey for an accolade that didn't matter. It was ridiculous. When he'd decided to give it up, Eli had spent an entire day thinking about what *he* wanted, not the script he'd tried to follow since birth. What were Eli's true measures for a successful life?

The answer had been easy to see with the gaping hole left in his heart. And it had nothing to do with ratings, apps, or the opinions of others. Eli was a good doctor—a great doctor already—awards or no awards. What Eli wanted was a happy family, a long life full of love, good work and adventures. Everything that Amara wanted, and he hadn't even realized it was the real prize.

Eli had had that life too. For a few blessed weeks, he'd had it. Until he'd let a simple comment by an irate patient's relative be the final thing that sent him spiraling out of control. It wasn't Mrs. Mora's fault. Eventually, his father, Griffin, a nurse, or some other stranger would have said something that made him want, so desperately, to prove them wrong.

That was what Eli had done so many times. He'd gone into emergency medicine because he'd felt it was his true calling. Then he'd immediately let Marshall's digs cause him to chase an acceptance that he doubted his father was capable of ever giving. Marshall's desire to be the best would always keep him from accepting a competitor for that title. Even if it was his own son.

The one person who'd never questioned his choices had been Amara. She'd offered him acceptance ten years ago and again when they'd reconnected. He'd never had to earn it—so it hadn't felt real.

That was the truth that burned him the worst. He'd thrown away the most real thing in his life. He'd always love her.

Always.

The doorbell rang, and Eli pushed his hands through his hair. He wasn't really presentable, but he doubted that was going to change anytime soon. "It's open," Eli called, not caring if the person on the other side of the door came in or left.

"Why is Griffin Stanfred's name on this survey and not yours?" Amara's voice was tired as she walked into the kitchen.

Eli shook his head and tried to figure out why Amara was here. His arms ached to pull her to him. To hold her, just one last time. It would never be enough, but he'd give almost anything for one more hug.

One more kiss, one more tomorrow.

Sucking in a deep breath, Eli shrugged. "The

hospital could nominate two physicians from every department. When I talked to Doug, I suggested that we put at least two names down in every category. Just being nominated is something that Griffin and the others can put on their résumé."

"That is not what I asked, and you know it." Amara scowled. "Why did *you*, Dr. Eli Collins, withdraw your name from contention? Was it because of me?" Her voice wobbled. "Were you punishing yourself?"

"Oh, honey. No." Eli stepped around the counter, but he still didn't reach for her. If he did, and she moved away, he wasn't sure he could survive that. "I did it for me, and for Griffin."

"For Griffin?" Amara blinked. "I don't understand."

"Griffin is looking to advance his career in a year or so. I'm not planning on leaving Boston Gen." Eli hesitated. "Unless you want me to?"

"No," Amara whispered.

That simple answer sent hope cascading through Eli's heart. "The nomination means more for him than for me."

"But it means the accolades, the acceptance,

go to Griffin too." Amara walked toward him. "You needed those."

Eli sighed. "No. I wanted them. So badly that I looked past the one person's acceptance who mattered most. And I lost her."

He took a chance and reached for Amara's hand. "I don't need to chase awards, love. I promise if any drop into my lap, I will happily accept them. But I want what I had and got too busy to enjoy. I want zoo days and dancing dates, vacations, morning snuggles and weird tea in the cupboard. I want all of it. And I will spend the rest of my life trying to show that to you if you will just give me a *second* second chance."

A tear slipped down Amara's cheek. "I never wanted you to not get all the awards." She hiccupped. "Or maybe I did. Because I was scared. I was so afraid that I'd get left behind that I never considered running beside you. That we could chase all our dreams together. I almost let fear chase away our happily-ever-after."

"Oh, honey—"

"No, let me finish, please." Amara wiped a tear away. "My father chased success, and my mom was alone, but that was her life. Not mine. I have been playing what-ifs for years. I thought it was so I could protect myself." She choked back a sob. "But I refuse to let fear cost me everything."

She put her hand on his cheek as she continued. "I want you to have every accolade, Eli Collins. And I want to be by your side as you collect them. I want to be your partner in everything. I love you."

"I love you too," Eli replied as his heart soared. His world righted as she held his gaze. This was life's top prize.

EPILOGUE

"IT'S HOT!" LIZZY complained as Amara held her hand.

"We'll be done soon," Amara promised. The head of the hospital stepped to the podium, and Amara smiled. Doug had sworn this would take no more than fifteen minutes.

"Up!" Lizzy said.

The three-year-old was having a rough time understanding why her constant growth spurts and Amara's growing belly meant that Amara couldn't hold her as long anymore. But she was being so patient today.

Just as she bent down to pick Lizzy up, Eli joined them. "Why don't you let me hold you, sweetie?" He kissed Amara's cheek as he lifted Lizzy.

Amara leaned her head against his shoulder and grinned. "Not that I'm complaining, but I thought Doug wanted you front and center for this?"

Eli laughed as he pulled at the collar of his shirt. "I told him I wanted the best seat in the house and standing back here is that location." He dropped a kiss across Amara's lips. "Besides, we'll see the banner better from here."

The *US News & Reports* team had sent banners to all the hospitals listed in the annual report. Amara had joked that it was a great marketing campaign for the magazine, and Eli had agreed. But it was a nice perk.

As the banner unrolled down the side of the hospital, Amara looked at Eli. It had taken a few years, but he'd made this possible. Her heart was full. "Happy?"

Eli stared at her and placed his free hand on her stomach, where their son was restless in the heat too. "Incredibly so." He kissed her before nodding toward the banner. "And it has nothing to do with that."

Amara laughed and gestured toward the bright blue words acknowledging Boston General as one of this year's Top-Rated Hospitals. "It's a nice bonus, though."

Eli chuckled. "It is."

* * * * *

LET'S TALK

For exclusive extracts, competitions and special offers, find us online:

 facebook.com/millsandboon

 @millsandboonuk

 @millsandboon

Or get in touch on 0844 844 1351*

For all the latest titles coming soon, visit millsandboon.co.uk/nextmonth